THE TIRED GUN

Lewis B. Patten

CENTER POINT LARGE PRINT
THORNDIKE, MAINE

This Center Point Large Print edition is published
in the year 2015 by arrangement with
Golden West Literary Agency.

The text of this Large Print edition is unabridged.
In other aspects, this book may vary
from the original edition.

Set in 16-point Times New Roman type.

ISBN: 978-1-62899-738-5 (hardcover)
ISBN: 978-1-62899-743-9 (paperback)

Library of Congress Cataloging-in-Publication Data

Patten, Lewis B.
The tired gun / Lewis B. Patten. — Center Point Large Print edition.
pages cm
ISBN 978-1-62899-738-5 (hardcover : alk. paper)
ISBN 978-1-62899-743-9 (pbk. : alk. paper)
1. Large type books. I. Title.
PS3566.A79T57 2015
813'.54—dc23
2015028543

Printed and bound in Great Britain
by TJ International Ltd, Padstow, Cornwall

MIX
Paper from
responsible sources
FSC
www.fsc.org   FSC® C013056

THE
TIRED GUN

Chapter 1

Western Kansas is a rolling country with a lot of low, rounded hills and watered draws and sometimes a little pocket of trees in one of them. That afternoon I halted my horse at the top of one of the highest of the hills and stared back in the direction I had come. I was all used up, half starved and beat, and I knew I was close to the end. Jess Morgan and his men had chased me a thousand miles and the chase had been going on for damn near a month. They had lost me twice, but both times had picked up the trail again. Now I faced the truth; I wasn't going to get away. And if I didn't get away, I was going to die.

I go by the name of Sam Court, after Jonathan Court, the Texas cowman who raised me. I never knew who my real folks were, but I suppose they were travelers who died along the trail. Near as I can tell, I'm thirty-three years old, and I guess you could say I'm fairly competent. But this time I'd sure bit off more than I could chew.

I couldn't see Morgan and his men, but I knew they were back there someplace, coming on as grim as death. They meant to hang me from the nearest tree or if there were no trees, from any hastily propped-up wagon tongue. I'd get some of them before they managed it, but both Morgan and I knew that I couldn't get them all. I couldn't get away and I couldn't win if I stood and fought.

Thinking about it, now that I figured death was close, I supposed that something like this had always been in the cards for me. At least since that day back in '68, eleven years ago when I took my drover's pay in Cottonwood Grove, Kansas, and used it to buy a gun.

Twenty-two I'd been, fresh up from Texas and mighty ignorant. It was the first time I'd ever been away and Cottonwood Grove was the biggest town I'd ever seen. But I was a man grown, or thought I was, and my pay was the first real money I'd ever had. I spent it on something I'd wanted for as long as I could remember.

Feeling a sudden chill and uneasy because of it, I turned my horse and rode east again. Maybe, I thought, if I hadn't bought the gun things might have been different for me. But I had bought it, and the last eleven years could not now be changed.

Our trail herd, a pool herd belonging to half a dozen different men, hit Cottonwood Grove in June of '68. It was one of the first to reach that town, the rails having been extended to Cottonwood Grove only the year before. I bought the gun and a lot of powder and ball and caps for it, figuring I'd learn how to use it right away. I had enough left for a room at the hotel for a week, some clothes, my meals and a couple of beers at the saloon. A week was all it took to make me decide that I didn't want to go back to that hot brush country ranch in southern Texas when the trail crew returned. Jonathan Court was dead. Without him I had no ties down there and nothing to draw me back. I decided to stay in Cottonwood Grove.

I took a job at the cattle pens, helping to crowd Texas longhorns into cattle cars. The work was hard, and dusty and hot, but it wasn't too much different from what I'd been doing all my life. And the wages were several times what I'd got from trailing north with the herd.

My horse stumbled suddenly, recovered and plodded on again. I thought glumly that I was going to have to have a new one before the day was out. And I needed food. Suddenly I wondered why I fought so hard. Sooner or later, death came to everyone. I'd seen other men die—before my own gun, and some of them had been even younger than I was now.

In the end, I thought bitterly, who was going to care if Sam Court died? Who, in all the world, would mourn for me?

Not my son, certainly, who was only six and who would not remember me if he even knew my name. He'd been only a squalling mite when I left Cottonwood Grove.

Six long years had passed since then, but even yet remembering hurt like the thrust of a knife. I

9

ached suddenly the way I had the day Nell died, The child had been to blame, I had told myself, because she had died bearing him. So after they buried her I went away, filled with bitterness and helpless anger because she had been the only one I ever really loved and, without reason, she had been taken away from me. I didn't ever want to see the boy again. I didn't want to see Cottonwood Grove, or anything else that would remind me and bring back that awful ache of loss.

Yet now, for some reason I didn't understand, I didn't feel that way any more. It hadn't been the boy's fault that Nell had died bearing him and I had been wrong to blame him for it. Her death had been something that just wasn't anybody's fault.

I hadn't paid much attention to where I was. When you're running, it doesn't matter much unless you're heading for some particular kind of country in the hopes of getting away. Now I realized I wasn't more than fifty miles from Cottonwood Grove. It was east and a little north. If I was a mind, I could reach it early in the morning, if my horse held out.

Realization that I was so close opened up a whole new bunch of thoughts. There was law in Cottonwood Grove and maybe the law could save my life. I'd killed Jess Morgan's brother, but it hadn't been a crime. It had been a fair fight and

Ray Morgan had drawn his gun and fired first.

Only you don't kill a Morgan and get away with it. Not up in the middle of Wyoming where the Morgan word is law. They owned dozens of square miles and controlled hundreds more. The ranch didn't even miss the score of men who were chasing me.

Then I shook my head. It wouldn't be fair to bring my kind of trouble into Cottonwood Grove. Even if there were twenty lawmen willing to fight Morgan and his men, it still would not be fair. And there weren't twenty lawmen. There was only one.

But they owed me something, I told myself stubbornly, all the time knowing it wasn't true. They'd paid me wages while I worked for them, and what I'd done had only been part of the job.

Yet still the pull of the past was there. I knew I was going to die and I suppose I wanted to see the town again before I did. I thought of the boy and I wanted to see him too. And Nell's parents, who were raising him, though I doubted if they'd want to see me very much. Particularly the way I was now, haggard and dirty and running for my life.

My horse had turned and was now headed straight for Cottonwood Grove. I had turned him myself without knowing it. Suddenly I made up my mind. I'd go back. I could at least get food, clothes and a bath. I could get a fresh horse. Maybe I could even get a couple of hours' rest.

And maybe I could make peace with what I knew was going to happen to me when Morgan and his men caught up.

The afternoon dragged on and no matter how I tried to keep memories from flooding back, I failed.

A green kid, I'd spent every spare moment I had practicing with my gun, which was a Colt's Navy Model .36-caliber. It was new and I remember thinking that it was the most beautiful thing I had ever seen.

It wasn't long before I could hit a tin can at fifty feet about four times out of five. And that wasn't bad for a gun never noted for great accuracy.

I used a piece of creek bottom about a quarter mile from town for my practice range because the town dumped their refuse there and there was a good supply of tin cans to use as targets. One day I was blazing away and I had the sudden, uneasy feeling I was being watched. I turned my head and saw a man sitting on a horse watching me.

I recognized him immediately as Ben Johnson, the town marshal. He was a stocky man of less than medium height with a broad, heavy-featured face. He wore a light colored flat-brimmed hat and he wore a vest over his fancy-ruffled white shirt. On the vest he wore his marshal's star.

But it was the way he carried his gun that interested me the most. He had a wide belt with loops in it, and the loops were filled with brass cartridges for his gun, which was like mine except that it had been converted to use rim-fire cartridges. There was a smooth leather holster on the right side, cut away so the gun would slip out easily when he needed it. The holster sagged from the gun's weight, low enough so that his hand didn't have to come up too high to close over the grips.

He said, "You're spendin' a lot of time at that. You're gettin' pretty good."

It embarrassed me, even though the man's tone told me it wasn't meant for a compliment. There was a moment's silence and then he said, "What you aim to do with the gun once you get good enough with it?"

I said, "Hadn't thought."

"Then what you practicin' so much with it for? Powder an' ball an' caps ain't exactly cheap, an' you work hard for what you get."

I said, "Man ought to be able to take care of hisself."

He shrugged. He stared speculatively at me for a few minutes. I could feel my face getting red. I kept staring back, my mind made up that I wasn't going to let him make me look away. Finally he said, "Want a job?"

"I got a job."

"An easier one. I need a deputy—someone to watch the jail when I can't be there. It's better than what you're doin'. Pays thirty a month an' a place to sleep."

I said, "I'll take it."

He nodded as if he'd known I would. He said, "Be at the jail at six o'clock tonight." And he turned and rode away without looking back.

I sat down on a dead cottonwood trunk and reloaded my gun. I was pleased to have got a better job and I didn't even think that I might be called upon to shoot at something besides tin cans in doing it. Neither did I see where it would lead me eventually or I'd have thrown that gun as far as I could and run all the way back to the loading pens.

I was down at the jail at six. Ben Johnson was putting on his hat and strapping his gun around his waist. He said, "Keep an eye on things," and just walked out.

I used the first money I earned as Johnson's deputy to buy myself a belt and holster. Instead of loops it had a powder flask that hung from it, a little box that held percussion caps and a leather pouch for bullets.

Ben Johnson was a cold man. He never smiled and he had no friends. There was a girl up at the Bulls Head Saloon that he sometimes took upstairs but it was obvious that she didn't like him and equally obvious that he wasn't overly fond of her. He just needed her periodically and his money was as good as anyone's.

When we were together in the jail office, he'd

sometimes talk. About the war. About the places he'd been. He'd been around most of the western part of the United States. He'd even been to Chicago once with a cattle train.

I asked him if he'd teach me to draw my gun as fast as he drew his and he said he would. After that, whenever we had a little time, he'd coach me and by the time spring came, I figured I was faster than anyone in town. When Ben Johnson suddenly refused to coach me any more, I figured I must be faster than he was, or at least as fast. He didn't want me to get any better than I already was.

The winter was hard and long and we were forced to stay inside most of the time, except for foraging trips along the creek bottom after wood. All the Texas cowhands had gone back home, so there wasn't much of a law enforcement problem any more. I worried about Johnson laying me off for the winter, but he never mentioned it. I finally decided he wanted me for next year when the trail herds would really begin to hit the town. He wanted me ready and available because he figured it was going to be more than he could handle by himself.

I practiced with the gun whenever I got the chance, and sometimes I'd catch Ben Johnson looking at me in a strange and speculative way, as if he was trying to guess what was going on in my mind. He seemed to get colder, as if he didn't like me any more, if indeed he ever had.

My horse stumbled several more times during the late afternoon and I finally got off and walked. I walked until dark. My stomach was cramping from hunger when I saw a dim light ahead of me.

It turned out to be coming from a small sod house. I rode into the yard and hailed the place and a man came to the door and asked me to come in. I dropped the reins and went inside.

I recognized him from when I'd been in Cottonwood Grove before, but apparently I'd changed so much that he couldn't recognize me. He was a kindly old man named Brunner, who had homesteaded here seven or eight years before. He didn't have much to eat, but he gave me what he had, some beans and a little sowbelly, and imitation coffee made out of roasted beans.

I felt myself getting sick, so I thanked him and hurried out. It had been so long since I'd eaten that my stomach just wouldn't hold all the food I had gulped as fast as I could.

I ran as soon as I got out the door, and I got a couple of hundred yards away before I vomited everything I'd eaten. Sweating and weaker than I could ever remember being in my life before, I mounted and headed for Cottonwood Grove again.

That moment, right then, was the low point of my life up to that time. For a while I didn't even care whether I lived or died.

Chapter 2

The sound of my horse's hoofs on the hard-packed road made a regular, monotonous cadence. Lulled by it, I dozed periodically, feeling safe in darkness as I never could in broad daylight.

As I drew closer to Cottonwood Grove where it had all begun and where it well could end, I couldn't keep my thoughts from returning to the past.

Ben Johnson had been cold and humorless and without friends, but never until the second summer did I suspect that he also was uncertain and sometimes afraid. His uncertainty and fear led him finally into an action that, indirectly, resulted in his death.

The first of the season's trail herds hit town in May. By the middle of June there were a hundred thousand cattle being held within ten miles of town awaiting their turn at the loading pens.

A hundred thousand cattle—forty or fifty separate herds, each with its complement of drovers who had spent three hard months on the trail. They wanted excitement. They wanted liquor, gambling, women and they liked to fight. Ten men in town from each of those forty or fifty herds added up to four or five hundred men. It was a madhouse—bedlam. In the evening there

17

were usually half a dozen fights going on simultaneously. Sometimes there'd be two or three gunfights in a single night.

Women weren't safe on the streets. Neither were the men who belonged in the town. I've heard all about Texans and their gallantry, but Texans are just like anybody else. There's good ones and bad, thieves and murderers and rapists as well as the old-fashioned, gallant kind.

They all became problems when they rode into Cottonwood Grove. And gradually, as the season wore on and as the waiting became more tedious, tempers became shorter and respect for Ben Johnson as the personification of the law turned into hatred for his inflexibility and arrogance.

It all came to a head on the night of July 4th. The day had been spent in celebration. Trying to channel some of the drovers' high spirits into nondestructive pursuits, the townspeople had arranged a picnic in the creek bed half a mile from town. Ten horse races were scheduled. Two steers had been barbecued and there were a dozen kegs of beer.

The townspeople tried hard to mix with the drovers, and in some cases it worked. Mostly it didn't. Fights began breaking out between towns-men and drovers, mostly over the drovers' attentions to the town women.

At six o'clock, Ben Johnson, his temper frayed by an afternoon of breaking up fights and jailing drunks, got up on the beer wagon and bellowed that the picnic was over and the drovers were to return to their herds immediately.

Johnson's tone betrayed his frayed temper and his announcement was greeted by catcalls and jeers. Watching him, I could see his face getting darker, could see the blood pounding in the veins on his forehead and in his neck.

Once more he bawled at the drovers to leave, this time even less diplomatically than before. More catcalls and jeers. And then one of the drovers yelled, "Let's shoot up the goddamn town!"

Immediately they scattered, heading for their horses. Ben Johnson ran for his own, with me close at his heels. But the drovers had a lead on us as they galloped out of the picnic ground and headed toward town.

We could hear the shooting long before we reached the town. When we did arrive, the scene that greeted us was almost unbelievable. The town's main street, called Kansas Street, was filled with milling cowboys on horseback. Most of them had guns in their hands, which they kept firing continuously at signs, at cornices on building tops, at windows. If the town hadn't been virtually empty someone would probably have been killed.

Ben Johnson had a double-barreled ten-gauge shotgun. He always kept it loaded with buckshot and today it was shoved down into a saddle scabbard. When we reached the edge of the mob, he withdrew it from the scabbard and fired one of the barrels into the air.

That ten gauge had a deep-throated roar entirely different from the crack of a six shooter. It boomed along the street and instantly got the attention of the mob.

I doubt if a man in that street suspected that Ben Johnson was afraid. He was as cold and stony as ever. The gun was steady in his hands, its muzzle trained on the nearest drovers. Only I could see how white Ben Johnson's knuckles were. Only I could see the knotted muscle along his jaw.

He roared, "Get back to your herds! You've got ten seconds and by God that's all!"

Someone yelled derisively, "Or you'll do what?"

"Or I'll fire this buckshot right into the middle of you!"

All of a sudden I was scared. Those Texans weren't about to be bluffed, and Johnson was scared enough to do exactly what he said he would. I said, "Ben, don't back 'em into a corner. Give 'em more time. An hour. Give 'em an hour to think it over."

He didn't say anything and he didn't look at me. It was as if he hadn't heard.

The seconds ticked away. Ben Johnson's jaw muscle relaxed and knotted again, even tighter than before.

I realized suddenly that he was really going to shoot. I opened my mouth to yell at him, but I was too late.

The shot boomed out, this time seeming a hundred times louder than the first shot had. Smoke rolled from the muzzle toward the nearest of the mounted men and before it had cleared, three of them were sliding out of their saddles, dead. Another four were crying out with the pain of their wounds.

I thought that mob would overrun and kill us then and there, but they did not. Sobered by what had happened, they sat their horses like they were paralyzed. Then, shocked and silent, they dismounted and carried away the dead. They helped the wounded toward the nearest saloon while others went to fetch the town doctor. Most of those remaining rode out of town, heading for their herds.

Johnson and I were left sitting our horses there, spectators only now. But I knew it wasn't over yet. When the shock wore off, when anger had time to build, they'd all be coming to Cottonwood Grove again. To wreck it or burn it to the ground.

Johnson went to the jail. I sat there in the street, shocked by what had happened, staring down at the pools of blood in the dusty street.

The townspeople began arriving from the picnic ground. They had stayed back while the shooting was going on but enough of them had seen what happened to tell the others and now everybody knew.

Several of them were panic-stricken. They said the drovers would attack and burn the town and that they weren't going to stay for it. They scattered and within ten minutes rigs piled high with hastily gathered belongings began rolling out of town, heading east.

I didn't want to go back to the jail. I didn't want to talk to Ben Johnson because I knew I'd give away how I felt about what he had done. I'd taken a job from him and I was his deputy, but I was really working for the people of the town, just as Johnson was.

I went into the nearest saloon and had a drink. I wasn't used to it, but right then I needed it.

The bar was crowded with townspeople, most of them the town's businessmen. They were trying to figure out what they were going to do to save their town. Marvin Levy, the mayor, wanted to ask for Johnson's resignation. He and some of the others figured if Johnson was fired, it would cool the cowmen's wrath.

Levy and three others left to go down to the jail. They were back before I finished my second drink. Johnson had refused to quit, they said. They also said he was as touchy as a teased rattlesnake.

Along about then they noticed me and their expressions brightened up a little bit. Levy said, "We want you to take over as marshal, Mr. Court." He called me mister because he knew it would make me feel big, but he didn't fool me one damn bit.

I hesitated, waiting to see what they'd say about the pay. Levy said, "We are paying Johnson a hundred and fifty a month, but you are pretty young." He tried to hold my stare and couldn't, and finally he said, "We will pay you the same if you can get rid of Ben Johnson before those drovers start tearing up the town."

I said, "I can get rid of Ben Johnson, all right, one way or another. Do you want me to kill him if he won't quit?"

Levy hemmed and hawed but in the end he agreed. I asked, "And what about the drovers? What am I supposed to do about them?"

"We will help you. We will back you up in whatever you decide to do."

I stared at him and at the others and I knew they'd run when the chips were down. I said, "I'll take care of it myself." I didn't know how I was going to deliver, but I sure wasn't going to let them know I had any doubts.

I've never seen a bunch of men so enormously relieved. They sagged with it. Levy said feelingly, "If you can get rid of Johnson and cool those Texans off, we'll make your salary two hundred a month for as long as you want to stay. And we'll be forever in your debt!"

I nodded. Even as young as I was, I suspected their gratitude would last about as long as a June frost, but I went out and headed for the jail.

Ben Johnson was pacing back and forth like a caged lion. He swung his heavy head and glared at me as I came in. "Know what those sonsabitches asked me to do?"

"I know," I said. "They asked you to quit."

"Then I guess you know what I told them."

"I know. So they sent me down to fire you."

He stared at me with disbelief. "You? Fire me?"

I said, "Mr. Levy has appointed me to fill your job. Give me the star."

He looked like he didn't believe his ears. He stared at me and for a minute I thought he was going to laugh. But he didn't. He roared, "You goddamn young whippersnapper, get the hell out of here!"

I said, "No, sir. I'm the new marshal. You get out of here."

He stared. "You're really serious!"

"Yes, sir. I'm serious."

He came toward me and I knew he was going to use his fists on me. If I let him do that, I'd get beaten badly, because I couldn't match his strength.

I'd never killed a man or even shot at one, but I supposed I'd always known that if you carry a gun and know how to use it well, eventually you will. I said, "No fists. Guns." I was steady enough

24

on the outside and I kept my voice from shaking, but inside I was scared to death.

He stopped. He stared at me for a long time and at last he said, "I guess I always knew it would eventually come to this."

I said, "Yes, sir. So did I."

"All right." He seemed to settle there. His hand tensed and his mouth drew tight. He eyes narrowed.

I looked for that telltale bunching of the muscles along his jaw. I saw it and suddenly I realized he was just as scared as I was.

Knowing that steadied me and give me confidence. I knew right then that I could beat him and I knew I'd kill him if he did not back off. But I gave him one last chance. I said, "It don't have to be like this, Mr. Johnson."

He shook his head. "Yes it does. You can't just let me walk out of here."

"No," I said. "I guess I can't. The townsmen thought if they fired you it would cool the cowmen off but I know better. The only thing that might cool them would be if you were arrested and tried for murder. So I got to put you under arrest. Unbuckle your gun belt and let it drop."

"You damn young whippersnapper . . . !"

I just looked at him. We stood there for several moments and then he made one last try at salvaging his pride. He said, "You first. I ain't going to draw on *you*."

I went for my gun, knowing he'd grab his the instant my hand began to move. And he did.

Well, I'd known I was fast but I hadn't realized how fast I really was. My gun was out, and level, and the hammer was back and my finger tight on the trigger before his even came level.

I could have fired, and almost did. Something stopped me. Maybe it was that I'd never killed a man before, but I can't really believe that was it. I think it was that I owed Ben Johnson some-hing. For teaching me. For hiring me. I didn't want to pay him off this way.

I didn't fire, and I risked my life by holding off because I gave him time to level his gun and pull the trigger. But he didn't. He froze, with the muzzle of his gun pointing at the floor at my feet and I saw the knowledge in his eyes that his life was in my hands. I said, "Let it drop, Mr. Johnson. I held off once, but if you raise it another inch you're dead."

His gun clattered to the floor. It was cocked and it fired from the impact but the bullet crashed harmlessly through the window.

I said, "Go back into that empty cell, Mr. Johnson. The charge is the murder of those three drovers."

He growled, "It'll never stick. I killed 'em in the line of duty."

I said, "Whether it sticks or not ain't up to me. Move!"

He looked at me in a way I can't describe and I wondered whether I hadn't done something worse to him just now than killing him. Then he turned and walked back to the empty cell, trying to look less beaten than he felt. He went in and I locked the door and pocketed the key.

I went back into the office. A dozen townsmen came crowding in. They'd been in the street and had heard the gun fire and had heard the window break. I said, "Ben Johnson is locked up, charged with the murder of those three men."

They backed out, looking at me with a mixture of unbelief and awe. The door closed and I sank down wearily in Ben Johnson's chair. I was the town marshal now and the problem of the drovers coming in to burn the town was my problem now. I'd have to figure out some way of handling it.

Chapter 3

The jail was full of drunks that Ben Johnson had arrested during the day. Most of them were fairly sober now. I went back into the corridor between the cells and said, "I'm going to turn you loose. Ride on out to your herds and tell the men there's nothing but trouble here if they try to get even for what Ben Johnson did. He's in jail and he'll stay there until he goes to trial for the murder of those three men."

I unlocked the cells and let them go. Ben Johnson did not look up, either at them or at me.

I washed and put on a clean shirt. Then I went back to Ben Johnson's cell and asked him for the marshal's star. He tore it off and threw it out through the bars. I picked it up and pinned it on my shirt.

I'd taken on a man-sized job. I didn't have any experience and I didn't have either age or reputation to help me out. I was going to have to prove myself. The next twenty-four hours would be the most crucial of my life. At the end of them I'd either be established as the town marshal or I'd be dead.

At sundown I made my rounds, the way I'd seen Ben Johnson do. The town was practically deserted, except for a few townsmen who were on the streets. The saloons were empty, the saloon-keepers standing out in front on the boardwalk smoking cigars and looking like they wondered what would happen next. They wanted the drovers back, but they didn't want to be burned out. I could tell that in spite of the way I'd managed to arrest Ben Johnson, they didn't think I could handle the job.

I went back to the jail. The streets grew dark. The saloons stayed open even though they had no customers. I could hear the nervous laughter of the saloon girls and once in a while the tinkle of a piano.

Night dragged on. I wondered when the drovers were going to hit. Probably at dawn, I decided, and I leaned back in the swivel chair and tried to get some sleep.

Levy came in. He said, "I couldn't sleep."

I got up, walked to the window and looked out. The streets were deserted. The clock on the wall said it was three o'clock.

Levy asked, "What are you going to do?"

"I'm going to try and stop them from burning your town."

"It's your town too."

"Yes, sir. It's my town too."

"But, how? How are you going to stop them? I know we said we'd stand back of you, but you can't count on any real help from us."

"I wasn't counting on it," I said.

He studied me. "I can't figure you out."

"There ain't nothing to figure out. You gave me a job to do and I'm trying to do it the best way I can."

"You know you might be killed?"

"Yes, sir. I knew that when I faced Ben Johnson."

"Aren't you afraid?"

"A man that ain't afraid of dying is stupid. But being afraid don't mean you got to run, or crawl."

He stared at me for several moments more. Than he shrugged, turned and went back out in the street.

29

I waited until he had disappeared. Then I went outside too. I stood in the doorway with the office dark behind me and I listened to the sounds of dawn. Birds began chirping and there was a fresh, clean smell to the air that you don't get any other time of day. The eastern horizon began to pale and pretty soon you could see the buildings across the street and finally you could see the railroad station and the loading pens beyond. The cattle crowded into them began to bawl and then I heard a low thunder that seemed to come out of the very ground beneath my feet.

I could see them in my mind, sweeping along like a charge of cavalry, maybe two or three hundred strong. And suddenly I was appalled at my own audacity. They'd roll over me as if I wasn't there. They'd take whatever vengeance would satisfy them on the town but they probably wouldn't completely ruin it because they still needed it. They needed the loading pens and the cattle buyers and they needed the saloons and the girls and the stores.

I thought about Ben Johnson's double-barreled ten gauge. I knew it would give me an edge, but I also knew that the sight of it would only anger the drovers more because it would remind them of what had started this. I left the shotgun inside and walked out into the middle of the street, with nothing but the Navy Colt's in the holster at my side.

My knees felt like water and my stomach felt like a great big hollow space. My chest was tight and I wasn't sure my voice would come out right when I did speak to them. If it didn't, if it broke or cracked, I was dead. Spread-legged I stood in the exact center of the street, looking toward that rumbling thunder of approaching hoofs, and waiting.

I could feel the eyes of the townspeople watching me. I could see, out of the corner of my eye, the girls clustered in the saloon windows and doorways. But there wasn't a soul upon the street.

Birds still chirped. Overhead a few thin clouds turned pink from the rising sun. I stood there like I was anchored to the dusty street. I'd wanted to run before in my life but never as much as I did that day. I knew if I moved I *would* run. I also knew if I had any sense I wouldn't be here when they swept on up the street.

Down beyond the loading pens I saw a huge cloud of dust, like that raised by a tornado, only this one had horsemen at its base. Only twenty or so of them were visible. The dust hid the rest from view.

They crossed the tracks, the sound of their horses' hoofs now filling the air so that you couldn't hear anything else. I knew they might ride right over me. They might not even stop. I might die under those pounding horses' hoofs without even being allowed to fight.

They couldn't have missed seeing me, but they did not slacken pace. They came on, filling the street, leaving it obscured behind them by the choking clouds of dust.

Half a block away, they had not even slackened pace. From one of the saloon doorways, a woman screamed. I flinched at the sound, but I didn't move. On they came, a wall of horsemen stretching from building to building across the width of the street. I didn't even know if they *could* stop in time. I only knew that, by God, they weren't going to make me run.

Now they weren't more than fifty yards away, and they still had not slowed down. In front I saw a grizzled oldster, whose bearing marked him their leader. He must have been close to sixty and the mark of power was plain on him. Just looking at him, even for an instant, you knew he was not only wealthy. You knew he was used to telling other men what to do and being instantly obeyed.

Six foot six he must have stood, though it was difficult to tell exactly how tall he was sitting on a horse. Gaunt and bony, but big of frame. His hair was a whitening lion's mane and his eyes were as blue as the bluest sky, yet possessed of a kind of fire that made it difficult to look away.

Twenty yards from me, he raised a hand. Both flanks of the moving body of horsemen overran him, but they stopped before they had completely encircled me.

Horses suddenly hauled in like that make a series of crow hops before they come to a complete halt. This man and his horse weren't more than a dozen yards away from me when they finally stopped. The man said, "Who the hell are you?"

"Sam Court. I'm the new marshal of Cottonwood Grove."

"Get out of the way, Sam Court! You're lucky we didn't run you down."

I said, "Ben Johnson is in jail. You've got no complaint against anyone but him and he'll stand trial for what he did. Go back to your camps. Or stay in town. But I want no trouble out of you."

He stared at me for a moment as if he didn't believe his ears. Then he roared with laughter. "You want no trouble out of us? Why boy, down home we eat your kind for breakfast every day!"

I said, "No you don't, because I'm from Texas too. Now you can either turn around and go back to your camps, or tie your horses and go into the saloons. But you do one or the other or by God get down off your horse and fight it out with me."

That sobered him. He asked, "How'd you manage to arrest Ben Johnson?"

"I outdrew him and he changed his mind."

He turned his head and stared toward one of the saloonkeepers, standing nervously in his open doorway. "That right?"

I said evenly, "Mister, if I said it, it's right."

Back in the crowd of horsemen somebody yelled, "What the hell are we waitin' for? Let's get at it!"

The big man roared, "Shut up!"

Another man laughed and asked, "Scared of that rooster, Mr. Burke?"

Right then I knew I was going to have to shoot it out with him. I didn't want to, but I wasn't going to get a choice. It was now a matter of pride with him and he couldn't back down any more than I could.

He said, "All right, son," and climbed down off his horse. He hitched at his gun belt to settle gun and holster snugly on his hip.

Behind him, the horsemen crowded hurriedly to right and left so as not to be in my line of fire. They left an open lane down the street directly behind Mr. Burke. I said, "You don't have to do this, Mr. Burke. All you got to do is give up wrecking the town."

He shook his head. "I've got to do it. You know that as well as I do."

I nodded. I knew, being from Texas myself, how strong pride was in men down there. I said, "I'm a lawman and I can't draw on you. If you want a fight, you got to draw on me."

He didn't like that very much and for a minute I thought maybe he'd give up on fighting me. Then someone in the crowd of horsemen yelled,

"Perforate the little rooster, Mr. Burke. Then we'll get busy doin' what we come to do!"

Burke moved. I could tell he was thinking that I'd outdrawn Ben Johnson and that Ben had been pretty fast. Burke was fairly fast for so big a man, but he wasn't nearly as fast as me. I waited until his gun cleared its holster before I even moved because I didn't want anybody saying later that I hadn't given him a chance.

Burke didn't quit the way Ben Johnson had. We fired simultaneously, but because he had hurried, Burke's bullet missed me clean. Mine didn't miss. It took him in the middle of the chest and he sat down suddenly in the dust of the street.

He remained sitting there, upright, for an instant before he toppled to one side. I knew that he was dead because I knew where my bullet struck.

I shifted the direction of my gun muzzle slightly until it covered the men nearest me. I said, "It was a fair fight and he forced it on me. Take him and get out of town."

Burke's death had sobered them more than I would have believed possible. Maybe it showed them where further violence would lead. Several of them got down and lifted him onto his horse. They tied him down so he wouldn't slide off and then they turned and rode back down the street, leading the horse with Burke's body on it.

Along the street, I could hear the collective

sigh of relief that came from the townspeople and the saloon girls. One of the girls began to weep hysterically.

I turned and went back into the jail. I didn't want praise for what I'd done. I'd kind of liked Mr. Burke and I'd had to admire him.

But now he was dead, and I was really the marshal of Cottonwood Grove. I was twenty-three and already I had begun building a name for myself.

Chapter 4

The townspeople made it plain how much they appreciated the fact that I had saved their town. Maybe they felt guilty because they hadn't stood behind me the way they'd said they would. Or maybe they really, honestly appreciated what I'd done. Anyway, they made me feel like a part of the town. They called me Mister Court when they spoke to me on the street, or they smiled and nodded as they passed.

The trail hands also treated me with respect. They still got drunk and they still wanted the same things they had before. But when I stopped a fight, it stopped. When I arrested a drunk, he came along without argument. And when I told a man to put away his gun, he put it away.

I must admit I enjoyed it. I made my rounds

three times a day. I stopped by each of the saloons at some time every day, sometimes drinking a beer, sometimes not. I rode out to the town dump every afternoon to practice with my gun. I enjoyed being who I was.

The summer passed, and eventually all the cattle were shipped east on the trains. The cowboys went back to Texas and the town settled down for the winter. Ben Johnson went to trial, was acquitted and left town right afterward, saying good-by to nobody and not even wearing a gun.

Now that the Texans were gone, the town began to have some social life of its own. There were dances at the Odd Fellows Hall. There were box lunch socials to raise money for the church. It was at one of these that I first saw Nell.

She was a tall girl, and slender. Her eyes were dark, her hair as dark as her eyes. They were auctioning her box lunch and it was going for fifty cents and she smiled at the man who had bid the fifty cents and suddenly I said, "A dollar."

The auctioneer looked a little surprised, but he went on, and the man who had bid fifty cents now bid a dollar and a half. I came right back with two.

Well, I got the box for three-fifty, and by that time Nell's cheeks were pink with embarrassment and everybody was laughing or smiling over the competition for it. I paid for the box and took it over to her and we went out onto the church lawn in the autumn sunlight. There were cottonwood leaves all over the ground and she spread a blanket and we sat down. Other couples were all around, but I couldn't see anyone but her.

I yanked myself back into the present savagely. I was shivering and cold. Remembering that first day with her was too painful to be endured. That afternoon had been the beginning of all that had been good in my life. Now Nell was gone, and the good was gone, and I was sick and cold and ragged and running for my life.

I got off my horse and walked. Gradually I began, at least, to get warm. But my head whirled, and sometimes I staggered, and at last I knew I'd fall down if I didn't get back on my horse.

I mounted, wondering how far back Jess Morgan and his men were. How long would I be able to stay in Cottonwood Grove? How long before they came?

The sky began to gray along the horizon in the east and gradually the light spread across the sky. I stopped my horse down by the loading pens in the cold gray light of dawn and stared at them.

Plainly they hadn't been used for years. They were coming apart and gray with age. Parts of them had been torn down by people wanting the lumber for firewood. The manure in the pens was dry as dust and finely powdered, but for an instant it seemed as though I could still smell rising dust and the reek of cattle and horseflesh and the mournful whistle of the trains.

I snapped back to the present, suddenly aware that I was really hearing the whistle of a train. Looking west, I could see its smoke and pretty soon it came around a bend in the track and I could see the train itself.

It was a passenger train, with five cars and a caboose. One of the times I'd lost Morgan and his men I'd done it by taking a train, but in the end they'd tracked me down. I knew it wouldn't do me any good to try a train again. The only way to get Morgan off my trail was to face him and if I faced him I'd be dead.

I'd never been a churchgoer, but Nell had been deeply religious. Her father was the Methodist minister in Cottonwood Grove. Now I wondered if maybe God wasn't taking retribution on me for some of the things that I had done. One of the commandments was, "Thou shalt not kill," and I doubt if there's room for argument about what it means. The commandment doesn't say, "Thou shalt not kill except in self-defense," or "except when you've got good reason or what seems like good reason at the time." It just plain means what it says and I'd broken it a good many times.

I stared up Kansas Street past the depot. The train was coming in fast so I crossed the tracks and stopped my horse.

There were half a dozen people on the platform to meet the train despite the early hour. A young girl about twelve got off, and was immediately embraced and led away by her mother and father. A salesman got off, carrying two heavy sample cases. He trudged away toward the hotel.

There were a few others, a husband, met by his wife, an oldster met by another man the same age. Two people were apparently disappointed, because when it became apparent no more passengers were going to alight, they turned and hurried away.

Nobody paid any attention to me, except for a quick glance or two. I didn't recognize any of those on the platform or any of those who had gotten off the train, but that wasn't surprising, I supposed. I'd been gone six years. Cottonwood Grove had grown. A lot of the old people had died or gone away. A lot of new people had come here to live.

The train sat there hissing. I rode on up the street, wondering now suddenly why I'd come. I didn't want people to see me like I was. Furthermore, I knew it wasn't fair to these people who had been my friends to bring my trouble home to them.

Well, I wouldn't stay long enough for Morgan to catch me here, I thought. I'd get a bath and a change of clothes and a fresh horse. I'd find some way of getting a glimpse of my son, and then

I'd go, without even letting him know who I was.

It came to me with a shock that I didn't even know his name. Nell had died bearing him and I'd left immediately, and he hadn't even been given a name unless Nell's father and mother had given him one, which no doubt they had. I wondered if they would have named him Sam, after me.

This lower end of Kansas Street once had been like a city in itself. There had been fourteen saloons running at one time, all of them filled to overflowing every night of the week when the cattle shipping season was in full swing. On the next street west there had been a line of sleazy bawdy houses. Looking at the backs of them across a vacant lot, I could tell they were empty now.

So were all but two of the saloons, their windows boarded up, paint cracking and peeling from their fronts. Out in front of one of the saloons, the Red Dog, a man was sweeping the boardwalk. I recognized him even from a distance of half a block. It was Hughie Blake.

He glanced up curiously when he heard my horse. He looked straight at me for several moments without recognizing me.

Hughie looked to be at least sixty-five. Six years ago he had been doing the same thing he was doing now, sweeping out the Red Dog every morning, washing the glasses, carrying out the empty bottles and the trash, cleaning and polishing the brass spittoons. He was a short man, and kind of dried up, but spry and hardworking and with a kind of salty humor that occasionally had a bite to it.

He breathed, "Mr. Court! Well I'll be jiggered! I didn't think I'd ever see you again!"

"Hello, Hughie. How are things with you?"

"The same. Same old town, same old job. You . . . Hell, get down, Mr. Court. The place ain't open for business yet, but that sure don't apply to you."

I slid off my horse and looped the reins around the rail. I knew I looked like hell; I could see it in Hughie's eyes. I felt like hell too. My stomach was scraping against my backbone and I was dizzy and weak. I staggered as I crossed the walk, but Hughie was ahead of me and didn't see, for which I was glad.

He knew I was hungry, though. First thing he did was go into the back room where the icebox was and fill me a big plate with cheese and cold sliced beef. He put a slab of butter on the plate, and a couple of big chunks of bread and brought it out to me. He drew me a mug of beer to go with it.

Remembering last night, I started slow, trying to forget how ravenous I was. I sipped a little beer after every bite.

As empty as I was, even that little bit of beer

went straight to my head. I began to feel a pleasant kind of lightheadedness.

Hughie pretended to be working behind the bar, polishing glasses, rearranging bottles, but I could feel him watching me. He didn't want to mention my leaving Cottonwood Grove because that would remind me of why I'd gone away. He was afraid to ask me how I'd been doing lately, because he could see. I supposed my reputation had spread back to Cottonwood Grove. I'd been involved in a lot of range troubles since leaving, and I knew how those things get blown up and exaggerated by the time they've been told a couple of dozen times.

I guess more to break the awkward silence than anything else, Hughie finally asked, "What you been doin', Mr. Court? And how come you're back . . . ?" He stopped, then added hastily, "I don't mean to pry, Mr. Court. I was just makin' talk."

I said, "It's all right. I've been a lot of places and I just happened to be within half a day's ride of here."

"Well, I'm sure glad to see you, Mr. Court. This town lost a lot when you went away."

I finished my beer and stared at him. He meant that. He meant exactly what he said.

I'd always been nice to Hughie, but I'd never thought of him exactly as a friend. Now, suddenly, I realized that was what he was. A friend. And a damn good one. He asked, "Want another beer, Mr. Court?"

I shook my head. Another beer and I'd fall down. He asked, "Some more to eat?"

Again I shook my head. I'd thrown up everything I ate last night, probably because I ate too much too fast. I wasn't going to make the same mistake today.

Hughie said hesitantly, "I'll bet you'd like some clean clothes and a bath, wouldn't you, Mr. Court?"

I nodded, thinking about it drowsily.

As if afraid I might take offense, Hughie said, "How would it be if I went and rousted up somethin' for you to wear? Just till you can buy some for yourself?"

I said, "I'd be grateful, Hughie. I've about wore these damn things out."

He hurried toward the door. "I'll be right back, Mr. Court."

I watched him go. I wondered what he'd say if he knew Jess Morgan and twenty men were chasing me and that if they rode in now they'd string me up right here.

I heard the train whistle and then heard it puffing as it pulled out of town. A quarter mile out, it whistled mournfully again.

It was quiet, then, so quiet you could have heard a match dropped clear across the room. Sun must have been touching the upper parts of the buildings on Kansas Street because there was suddenly a warm, yellow light inside the big saloon.

I looked down at my clothes. One boot was split open where the upper joined the sole and part of my ragged, dirty sock stuck out. Both boots were run over at the heel and had holes in the soles from walking and leading my horse so much.

My gray woolen Confederate Army pants were torn in half a dozen places from the heavy brush I'd ridden through. They were filthy and although I couldn't smell myself I didn't doubt but what others could. I had a gray homespun shirt that a good-hearted homesteader woman had given me. It was faded from many washings and stained with sweat, and it was torn half way down the back. My underwear was the only thing I had that wasn't full of holes and I hadn't had it off for a couple of weeks.

I was carrying a different gun. This one was a Colt's .44 single action that used rim-fire cartridges. The loops in the belt were full of them, some of the cases green with corrosion. My hat was a shapeless, wide-brimmed Confederate Cavalry officer's hat, stained around the band with sweat and brown with dust.

I wondered if Hughie had suspected that I couldn't buy new clothes because I didn't have the money. Maybe he had. It had been eleven years since I turned to the gun and all it had got me was what I had on, a beat-up saddle that wasn't worth more than two or three dollars, a horse that would turn up his toes if I rode him ten miles more and a gun, the smooth-gripped, carefully oiled tool of my trade. In my pocket I had eight dollars and seventy-three cents and somehow I had to make that do for a horse trade. I had to have an animal that would get me out of here before Morgan and his men arrived.

I finished the last swallow of beer in the mug and got to my feet. I walked to the doors and stared out into the street.

I should have stayed, I thought. And suddenly I was remembering again.

Chapter 5

Each of the empty saloon fronts along the street brought its special memory, and some of them brought dozens, crowding in upon each other so rapidly that my mind could not keep up. I began thinking about Hughie Blake and suddenly I remembered something that explained Hughie's warm and unexpected friendliness toward me. I'd almost forgotten it in the press of years, but now it was back, as clear and plain as if it had happened yesterday.

Three buffalo hunters were in town. They were

as different from the Texans as night from day. They stank of death as well as from a dozen other things and they were a wild and hairy lot that other men avoided if they could. If they stood at the bar, there'd be a space six feet wide on either side of them, and saloons had a way of emptying when they came in.

They had to have resented it. They could have changed it just by cleaning up but I suppose they were too stubborn to do that.

Hughie was working all day then. It took a man full time just to keep the place presentable. I wasn't in the saloon when the ruckus started, but I guess Hughie swept around the buffalo hunters, keeping a distance of six feet or so and they made him the goat for all the anger and resentment they felt toward the Texans for avoiding them.

When I got there, they were holding Hughie down on the floor. They'd deliberately upset a spittoon and they were shoving Hughie's nose into the mess the way you'd shove a dog's nose into something he's done on the floor as a way of housebreaking him.

I didn't like the three much anyway and as I walked into the saloon and saw what was happening, suddenly I saw red. For once, I completely forgot that I had a gun.

One of the three held a rifle to keep the other men in the saloon from butting in. I hit him with my shoulder and slammed him into the bar so hard it rocked on its base and spilled drinks all down the length of it. Before he could recover, I grabbed the rifle and brought it up, hard, against his throat.

It must have collapsed his windpipe, because I'd never seen a man get so sick so fast. He choked as if something had completely stopped the air going into his lungs. He lost interest in both the rifle and what was going on. He bent double, gasping and retching and heaving with his chest as if he was going to die if he didn't get a breath.

I had wrenched the rifle away from him. One of the other hunters looked up from what he was doing to Hughie and I let him have the butt of it right in the mouth. It smashed all his front teeth and made a bloody mess of his mouth. He backed off, his hand going for the long-barreled pistol he had in his belt. I cracked him across the forearm with the barrel of the rifle and I could hear the bone snap in his arm.

The third hunter, struggling with Hughie, who was sobbing with frustrated fury and disgust, suddenly slipped on the slimy floor. I turned from the second one and put my foot down on the back of his neck, shoving his face into the mess he'd been trying to shove Hughie in. I said, "Get out of here, Hughie, and get yourself cleaned up. These three have just decided to leave town."

The one on the floor grabbed my leg and tried to dump me. I brought the butt of the rifle down on the top of his head and his face went right back down into the mess on the floor.

I looked over at the bartender. I said, "Get some mops and a bucket. These boys are going to clean up the mess they've made."

And clean it up they did. With a broken arm and a mouthful of smashed teeth, the second one worked with his good arm, never once looking up. The first one, still gagging, rolled his unconscious friend out of the mess and helped. When it was done, they dragged the unconscious one out. The gagging one was breathing better now. He went after the wagon that they'd used to come to town. The two threw the unconscious one in the wagon and they drove out of town without even bothering to look back. I don't know what happened to them because I never saw them again. Hughie Blake thanked me for what I'd done later, but I didn't pay too much mind. To me, it was just a part of the job. I guess to Hughie it had been more than that.

The doors opened and I turned. Marv Levy stood there, looking just like he always had, stooped, wearing gold-rimmed glasses, black sleeve protectors, a threadbare vest and pants that were shiny on the seat. He was a little more bald than when I had seen him last, and maybe a little more stooped. He crossed the room and peered nearsightedly at me, nodding as he did. "Yes. Yes, it is you. I am glad you have come back."

I grinned. He looked me up and down and then he asked, "Is the law after you? What have you done?" I shook my head. "The law isn't after me."

He released a sigh of relief. "Good. Good. That is good."

We stood there looking at each other for several moments, neither knowing what to say. Finally he said, his tone almost fatherly, "Sam, you don't look so good. You're thin. You look like you been traveling hard. *Somebody* is after you?"

There wasn't any use in beating around the bush. I said, "Man named Morgan. Jess Morgan. I shot his brother up in Wyoming more than a month ago. He's been chasing me ever since."

"Shot him? Killed him, you mean?"

I nodded.

"It was self-defense?" he asked hopefully.

I nodded again. "Yes. It was self-defense. The man picked a fight with me and he wouldn't let me get out of it."

"Then this Morgan, he is wrong, is he not?"

"He's wrong, but that won't keep him from stringing me up from the nearest tree when he catches up with me."

Levy was silent a moment, turning this over in his mind. At last he said, a bit doubtfully, "This town . . . all of us owe you a debt. You saved the

50

town from the drovers the first year you were here. You saved my store from them when they would have burned it. We will stand back of you. We will not let this Morgan do anything to you."

I stared at him. I could see his hands trembling. He was scared, but that hadn't kept him from doing what he thought was right. Trouble was, he was only one. The rest of the town wouldn't stand behind what he had promised me.

I put out my hand and gripped his shoulder. "Thanks, Mr. Levy. I appreciate that. I really do." I was kind of choked up myself over his unexpected offer of support even if I couldn't count on it.

He said, "I will fetch the marshal. We will get people together. How long do we have?"

"Today. Not more than that and maybe less."

"They are that close?" He was even more scared now than he had been before. He whirled suddenly and scurried out of the saloon.

I watched him go. I thought about Jess Morgan, big and wild and used to doing just as he pleased. I thought about the twenty men he had with him. They could take on this town as easily as Quantrill's raiders had taken on Lawrence during the war. Resistance against them would not only be useless; it would be stupid too.

I went to a table and sat down, feeling dizzy and weak. The food I had eaten made a hard lump in my stomach and the beer had made my head

51

whirl. There was no use getting my hopes up. My situation was just as hopeless now as it had been last night. If I didn't run, Morgan would catch me here and I would die where all my friends and my son could see.

After that, how would it be for him, growing up in a town that had seen his father hanged? It wouldn't matter that I would have been hanged unlawfully. In time, people would begin to say, "He must have been guilty or those men wouldn't have hanged him. You don't string a man up for nothing. No, sir, you don't."

I got up and began nervously pacing back and forth. I stopped and stared out the door. I could see the front of Levy's store and the big sign over it, LEVY'S HARDWARE AND MERCANTILE. EST. 1865. Suddenly I remembered the day the drovers had almost burned it for him.

That year, because of an early spring, the herds came up the trail before either the town or the railroad was ready for them. They bunched out on the prairie, waiting for scarce cattle cars, waiting for their turn at the loading pens.

The drovers didn't have any money and the cattle buyers weren't willing to advance any until they were sure cattle cars were going to be available.

Levy extended them credit for a while. He even advanced money on their signature, just as he had in years gone by. He refused credit to one trail boss, a Texan named Garth, who had not paid him several hundred dollars owed from the year before. Infuriated at being refused, Garth and half a dozen of his drovers, drunk enough to be reckless, broke into Levy's back door, intending to burn the place after taking what they wanted from his shelves.

I happened to see the glow of a match as I passed the place, making my regular rounds. And I smelled coal oil.

I suppose if I'd had any sense, I'd have gone for help. But that match and the smell of coal oil told me I might not have time for that. I smashed the door glass with my gun, reached in and unbolted it, and ducked inside.

A volley of shots racketed from the back part of the store. They shattered the front windows. Back in the darkness, someone yelled, "Come on. Light the damn thing and let's get out of here!"

Another match flared. This one was thrown on the floor and a pool of flame began to spread from it.

I knew in another instant the whole thing would be aflame. I also knew if I ran into the light from that spreading pool of fire, they'd cut me down like a duck in a shooting gallery.

But in those days, I didn't always use my head. I just did things. That night I jumped up and ran down the long aisle toward the fire growing at its end.

They opened up on me. I made a perfect, well-lighted target. The only thing that saved my life was the speed with which I ran.

One bullet tore through the muscles of my upper arm. Another entered my thigh in front and came out in the back. Still another creased my head.

That third bullet probably saved my life. It stunned me long enough to make me fall, and the rest of their bullets ripped through the air directly over me.

I began firing from the floor at their gun flashes, and I heard one man yell and heard another slammed against some piled-up barrels, bringing them crashing to the floor. Then they were gone and I was alone with the fire, which was crawling rapidly toward me.

Blankets were piled high on a nearby counter. I grabbed some of them and smothered the fire with them, getting myself pretty badly burned doing it.

It was out by the time Levy and the other townspeople came streaming in the door. One of the drovers was dead, another wounded in the arm. He told them who the others were and a posse of the townspeople went out and arrested them. I was in bed for a couple of weeks, and I hobbled around for a couple of months. Marv Levy was so grateful it was embarrassing. His wife used to bring me rich Jewish dishes almost every day.

Now, I thought, he was going to back me, protect me from Morgan because he thought he owed it to me. And he didn't. I'd been marshal, and protecting his store had just been part of the job.

Chapter 6

Hughie Blake came back shortly after Levy left with a bundle of clothes in his arms. He laid them down on a table apologetically, saying in a halting voice, "They're the best I got, Mr. Court. They ain't much, but they're the best I got. They'll be too small but I think you can get 'em on."

I looked at the clothes, a pair of shiny black trousers from his Sunday suit and a clean white shirt, as well as a suit of red flannel underwear and some socks. I didn't want to take them but I knew it would hurt him if I refused. I said, "I appreciate it, Hughie. I really do. I guess I look like hell."

"No, sir, Mr. Court. You look just fine. I just thought maybe you'd want somethin' to wear, at least while yours is gettin' washed."

"I doubt if there'll be time for that."

"Oh yes, sir. I know a woman who'll do 'em right away, just as soon as you get 'em off. They'll be ready before noon." He looked embarrassed. "Not that I'm tryin' to hurry you . . . I mean . . ."

I said, "It's all right, Hughie. I know what you mean."

The sun was up, casting shadows in the street. On the other side a man unlocked the door of the barbershop and went in. He was Glen Sanchez, a slight, dark-haired, dark-skinned man, half Mexican. He came out right away and crossed the street to the saloon. He came bursting in, his dark eyes searching back and forth until he saw me standing there. Then a grin spread across his face and his teeth flashed. "Mr. Court! I heard you was back." He crossed to me and put out a hand. I gripped it but it was a moment before I could speak. I said, "Hello, Glen. It's been a long time. How you been?"

"Fine! Fine! Nothin' ever changes around here."

He peered at me, started to say something, then hesitated. I grinned. "You're right. I do need a shave. Haircut too."

Glen said, "Come on, then. I just opened up."

He went out and I followed him across the street. I only had a little over eight dollars and I had to have a fresh horse, but I didn't want Nell's parents to see me looking the way I did. I followed Glen into his shop with its faint lingering odors of shaving soap and bay rum. I was carrying the clothes Hughie had brought me.

56

When Glen saw them he asked, "Want me to heat water for a bath?"

"Uh huh. Just as well do the thing up right."

Glen went into the back room. I could hear the lids of the stove and the noises he made building a fire in it. I sat in the barber chair and leaned back. I closed my eyes. The pump began squeaking and buckets banging as Glen carried in water to fill the big wash boiler on top of the stove.

I dozed I guess. When I awoke the sun had changed position and I knew I must have slept close to an hour. Glen was sitting on the customers bench reading a newspaper. He glanced up as I raised my head. "You must've been plumb wore out. Bath's ready any time you are."

I got up and went out back. Sanchez dipped hot water out of the boiler with a bucket and poured it into the wooden tub. He cooled it with water he carried in from the pump and tested it with his hand. I pulled off my boots and took off my clothes. Glen took my dirty clothes out, I suppose to carry them across the street so that Hughie Blake could have them washed.

For a little while I just soaked in the hot water. Then I thought of how close Jess Morgan was and I began to wash. It had been more than a month since I'd had a bath and I needed it. With my clothes off I could see how much weight I'd lost. My ribs stuck out and my belly was hollow.

My legs were thinner than they'd ought to be.

As soon as I'd finished, I got out and dried on the towel Glen had left for me. I dressed in Hughie's clothes and picked up my holstered gun from the floor beside the wooden bathtub where I'd left it when I got in to bathe. I strapped it on and pulled on my worn-out boots and went back out front and crawled into the barber chair.

I hitched around so my gun would be exposed. Glen started to put the chair all the way back so he could shave me but I said, "Huh uh. Leave it up. I've got to be able to see the street."

Instantly his face clouded. "You in trouble, Mr. Court?"

I said, "Yeah. I guess you could call it that."

"Anything I can do?"

"Not unless you're willing to take on twenty men."

He whistled. "That bad, huh?"

I didn't answer. After a moment he asked worriedly, "The law, Mr. Court?"

"Worse. This one is the self-appointed law over a hundred square miles of Wyoming land. He thinks he's God."

He lathered my face and put a hot towel over it, not covering my eyes. I could tell he wanted to ask me what I'd done to have Morgan after me but was afraid. I said, "I killed his brother. It was a fight that he started, but right or wrong don't make any difference to Jess Morgan. Not when his brother has been killed."

"Can't *you* go to the law?"

"What law? Up there the law supports members of the Cattlemen's Association no matter what they do."

"Then here. Tell Jellico about it. He's the new marshal. Has been since you left."

"Morgan would kill him."

"Then what are you going to do?"

"Keep going, I guess. Maybe he'll eventually get tired and quit." He wouldn't, but it was my problem, not Glen Sanchez's.

"You got a lot of friends here, Mr. Court."

"Thanks, Glen."

"They'll help. I'll help. All of us will."

"And get shot up. Or have your town burned."

"You kept that from happenin' once, Mr. Court. If you hadn't stood up to them drovers I wouldn't have a shop. Maybe I wouldn't even be here."

For some reason I couldn't understand, his answer irritated me. I said shortly, "It was part of the job. You don't have to go on feeling grateful forever just because of it."

He was silent a moment and I could tell my sharp reply had hurt him. Then he said, "It ain't that, Mr. Court. We're your friends."

I said, "It was a mistake coming back."

"No, sir. No it wasn't. Man needs help and he

goes where his friends and family are. Your son—
he's a fine boy, Mr. Court."

I stared into the street. A couple of boys were
standing on the far side staring in through the
window of the barbershop at me. Their faces
had an awestruck look that I'd seen at other times
in other towns. I was Sam Court, the famous
gunfighter and the stories going around had me
the killer of twenty men, not counting Indians.

Out in the street, one of the boys, who must
have been ten, yelled up the street, "Hey, Billy!
It's Sam Court! He's right here in the barbershop!"

Another boy showed up, running. The first one
pointed at me and all three stared intently through
the window of the barbershop. Gaining courage,
they inched across the street, poised as if ready
to run at the slightest movement from me.

Sanchez said, "Looks like you got some
admirers, Mr. Court."

"Looks like."

The boys came right up to the window and put
their noses against the glass. I said, "My boy . . .
what's his name?"

"You don't know? I'd a thought . . ." He
stopped.

I said, "My wife . . . her dying . . . it hit me. I
haven't written."

"Well, his name's Jonathan. You're goin' to see
him, ain't you, while you're here?" He finished
shaving me and put a hot towel over my face,

leaving it clear of my eyes so that I could see. I didn't have to answer because of the towel.

Two more boys showed up out in front. Sanchez finished with my face and pinned a hair-cutting cloth around my neck. He got his scissors and comb and went to work.

The five boys staring in through the window embarrassed me. Sanchez asked, "Want me to run 'em off?"

"Huh uh. They're not hurting anything." I closed my eyes.

Suddenly, as clear as if she was standing in front of me, I could see Nell's face. It was the first time in several years I'd been able to.

Nell hadn't liked the way I made my living from the first. She'd wanted me to go into something else, to put away the gun. Her father offered to loan me five hundred dollars to start a store or buy one that was already here.

I'd told her I didn't want to. I said I was good at what I did and I said the town needed a marshal who could keep the peace. I could, and there wasn't anybody else in town to take my place.

Her face faded from my memory as suddenly as it had appeared and however hard I tried to bring it back I failed.

After that first time, she never complained about what I did again although I was sure her father and mother kept hammering away at her over it.

Four years we were married. Thinking back and remembering, it seemed more like four days. Or four weeks at most. The days fled by and I was happier than I had ever been before. We both wanted children but for a long time it didn't look as though we would ever have any.

Then Jonathan came along. There was no reason to believe everything wouldn't be all right. Nell was healthy. The doctor said everything was fine.

Except that it wasn't fine. I heard the baby cry upstairs and I waited and waited for the doctor to come tell me whether it was a boy or girl but when he came down he didn't say anything about that. He looked grave and sad, and he said, "I'm afraid I've got bad news for you."

Even then it didn't register. I said, "The baby died?"

"No," he said. "The baby is all right. And a fine boy he is."

"Then what . . . ?" I saw it in his face, in his eyes and I shoved him aside and raced up the stairs. I went down on my knees beside her bed and I gathered her into my arms as though I could breathe life back into her.

But she was already growing cold. I looked across at the tiny mite of a baby lying in the cradle we'd bought for him and I hated him. Small and helpless as he was, I hated him.

I turned back to Nell, ignoring the baby's

whimpering, and I felt myself convulsed. Tears scalded my eyes. But it wasn't any use. Nell was gone and it was like all my reason for living had gone with her.

The doctor came up and tried to pull me away but I wouldn't budge. He went and got help, and between them all they got me to leave her. When I did they covered her face with a sheet. The doctor gave me a bottle and only after I had finished it and had passed out did they take her body away from our house.

I was sick and empty and hopeless at the funeral. People, including Nell's father, told me that the living must go on. They told me I had a son to live for now, as if that tiny mite of a baby could ever replace Nell.

I didn't see the baby again. That night I got my horse and rode away. I hadn't written since and I had not been back until today.

Sanchez finished cutting my hair. He brushed me off and I got out of the chair. The boys stepped away from the window, as if getting ready to run when I came out. I fished in my pocket to get money to pay Glen Sanchez, but he put his hand on my arm. "Do you think I could take money from you, Mr. Court? Not in a million years!"

I should have stayed here, I realized now. I'd had friends in Cottonwood Grove, and I'd had a son. If I'd stayed, I wouldn't now be the famous or infamous Sam Court. I wouldn't have left such a trail of dead men behind me and I wouldn't now be running for my life.

I thanked Glen Sanchez and stepped out onto the boardwalk in front of his shop. I still had my old worn-out boots on and my battered Confederate hat, but I was clean, and shaved, and I felt a lot better than I had before. I'd even had an hour's nap.

The boys stood there gawking at me. I took a dime out of my pocket and tossed it to one of them. I said, "Take my horse down to the livery barn, will you, boy? Tell Karl Bruce I'll be down later to trade him out of another one."

"Yes, sir, Mr. Court." The boy, followed by his friends, raced across the street to where my horse was tied. He untied the reins and led the animal toward the livery barn.

The horse plodded along, head down, as though he might fall at any time. I wondered how he'd ever managed to come this far.

Chapter 7

For a moment I stood in front of the barbershop watching the five boys lead my horse away. The sun was now high enough to fill the street with sunlight. A buckboard went by, driven by a man I didn't know. He glanced at me, then glanced

64

incuriously away again. There were probably a lot of people in Cottonwood Grove that I didn't know, I thought. Six years is a long time to be away, and a lot of things are bound to change.

Something made me glance up the street. I saw a man approaching, a man I immediately recognized. He was tall and thin. His shoulders were a little stooped. He wore a black suit, the seat and elbows of which were shiny from wear. The pants were baggy at the knees. He wore a white shirt and black tie, and a black, broad-brimmed hat like the ones worn by Quakers I had seen.

It was Jasper Prouty. He had heard I was in town and now he was coming to tell me to leave without seeing my son. I knew it even before he was close enough to speak.

Watching him come down the street suddenly brought a memory of him standing at the altar of the little white Methodist church while Marv Levy, Nell's godfather, led her down the aisle. I'd never seen Nell's father without that black, shiny suit. And it suddenly came to me that I'd never seen him laugh. The closest he ever came to it was a small, frosty smile. It was possible he was warmer with his family than with others, but I doubted it.

I thought suddenly that this was the man to whom I had entrusted the raising of my son. When he was close enough he gave me a small, grudging nod. "I heard you were in town."

I didn't answer him, because I didn't know what to say. He was silent for several moments and at last he asked, "Will you be staying long?"

I could have told him no. I could have told him I was leaving shortly after noon, before the men who were pursuing me arrived. But I didn't. I said, "I haven't decided yet."

His face was thin and sharp. His lips were pale, his cheeks hollow, his nose long and straight. His hair was the color of a slate sky in wintertime.

He studied my face. I hoped he couldn't tell from it how I felt. Despite the bath, the shave and the hour's nap in the barber chair, I still felt terrible. I was exhausted. I was sick at my stomach from the food and my head was still light from that single beer. I wanted nothing so much as to crawl into a clean bed and sleep the clock around. But I wasn't going to get the chance.

He said, "You gave him up. You left without even seeing him."

I nodded. "I know."

"He doesn't know about you. We haven't told him."

"His name is Court. How can he help but know?"

"His name is not Court. It is Jonathan Prouty. And I don't want him to know." His eyes were cold and unfriendly.

"Why?"

"A father should be an example to his son. He should give his son some cause for pride."

"And I don't?"

"Word of your exploits reaches even a little place like this. You are talked about in the saloons. They say you have killed twenty men."

"And you believe it?"

"Why should I not believe it? Such stories do not invent themselves."

"You don't like me much, do you?"

"No, I do not. I detest you and all you stand for."

"And you want me to go away?"

"I want you to go away. Now." He let his eyes touch my worn-out boots and battered hat. The clean clothes didn't fool him. He knew somebody had loaned them to me. He said, "If you need help . . ." He fished in his pocket for the long, leather pouch in which he carried his money.

Before he could get it out, I said harshly, "No."

"Why not? Nell would have wanted me to help you if you needed help."

He was beginning to anger me, but I kept myself under control. That was one thing I had learned. When you carry a gun and use it well, you have to keep control of yourself. Otherwise you're no better than a rabid dog. I said, "I don't know how you managed to raise a girl like Nell."

"What do you mean by that?"

"Just that she was everything you are not."

"I wasn't the one who ran off and left the boy."

I started to answer, then stopped myself. We were standing here bickering after six long years, and bickering wouldn't change anything—my feelings toward him or his toward me. I said, "I want to see my son."

"No!" There was something close to panic in Prouty's eyes.

I said, "I intend to see him, no matter what you say. That is my right. I am his father."

"Father!" Prouty spat the word at me. "It takes more to be a father than . . ." He stopped, clenching his fists at his sides. He was trembling with emotion, but I couldn't tell whether that emotion was hatred toward me or fear that I might take the boy away from him.

I said, "I want to see my son."

"And tell him who you are? Tell him you are Sam Court, the killer?"

"He'll find out sooner or later."

"Maybe not. Maybe I can keep it from him."

I shook my head. "Not a chance. I'm surprised you have so far. If you really have."

"I have all right."

I said, "Not everybody in this town thinks I'm a killer. A lot of them remember me as the man who saved their town and some of their lives."

"That was before you went away. You can't

68

deny that since then you've made your living by your gun."

I said, "That don't make me a killer." I was startled to realize that I was trying to justify myself to him. As if I wanted his approval.

He said, "A killer is one who kills."

Wearily I said, "All right, Mr. Prouty. Have it your way. But you can't stop me from seeing my son."

All the arrogance, all the disapproval suddenly was gone from him. His shoulders sagged. He started to speak, then stopped and swallowed as if the words would not come out. And there was a scared look to his eyes. Finally he said in a hoarse and halting voice, "You raise a child from a baby and he's like your own. We lost our child when Nell died, but it was like God gave us Jonathan to take her place. Don't take him away from us. Please don't take him away from us."

For a moment I stared at him. All the stiff, self-righteousness was gone and there remained only a man who loved a little boy. I realized that Jonathan could do worse. This was a side of Prouty I had never seen before. It explained how he had been able to raise Nell to be the kind of girl she was. I said, as gently as I could, "I didn't come to take him away from you. I just came to see him. I don't even care if he sees me."

Relief so strong it left him shaking came over Prouty. He turned his head and rubbed his eyes.

When he turned back to me there was an unexpected humility in his face. "I am sorry. Of course you can see him."

I waited. He said, "Come with me." He turned and headed back up the street toward the church.

The five boys who had taken my horse to the stable had returned. They stood in a group watching me from about a hundred feet away. When I walked away with Prouty, they followed.

We went up Kansas Street to the second intersection and then turned right. The sky was an almost unbelievable blue, with puffy white clouds floating in it. The sun was warm on my back. It had been on such a day that Nell and I had been married.

Suddenly I was scared. I didn't want Jonathan to see me. I didn't want him to know who his father was. I didn't want him to be like those boys back there, all but worshiping me because of my ability to use a gun, because of the men I had faced and killed.

I stopped and looked back at the boys. I beckoned them.

They approached fearfully, the one I had paid to stable my horse being the boldest of the five. I fished in my pocket and found a quarter. I said, "How'd you boys like to go down and get a nickel's worth of candy each?"

The one who had stabled my horse found his voice first. "Gee, Mr. Court, that'd be great!"

I tossed the quarter to him. "Go on, then. A nickel for each of you."

He caught the quarter. He said, "Thanks, Mr. Court," and the others echoed him. Turning, the five raced back toward Kansas Street. They disappeared around the corner.

We turned up the alley behind the church. I remembered that the parsonage was beyond, on the other side of it.

Prouty halted beside the stable in back of the church. He said, "Wait here. I'll bring him out the back door of the house. I'll tell him I need help with something in the church."

I nodded. My throat felt as if it was closed and I didn't trust myself to speak. Prouty looked at me strangely, then turned and went on up the alley to the back gate of the parsonage.

I felt cold. My knees were shaking. I was glad nobody was around to see me because right now I didn't look much like Sam Court was supposed to look. I watched the back door of the parsonage more intently than I could remember watching anything before. At last I saw movement behind the screen door and I realized I was holding my breath.

I let it slowly sigh out as the screen door opened. A little boy came out, hurrying. He jumped down the three steps to the ground, then turned and looked back eagerly.

He was dressed in overalls, faded and out at

both knees. He had on a blue shirt that looked a little small for him, and his straw-colored hair hadn't seen a barber's shears for a month.

I wished I was closer so that I could see his face better. I stared intently, knowing that this short moment was all I was going to get and trying to fix him forever in my memory, the way his mother was.

I saw Prouty looking toward me, saw him gesturing for me to get back, and I realized I was exposed. I drew back quickly, relieved that I had not been seen. Jonathan ran toward the back door of the church with Prouty following. He disappeared inside.

Prouty glanced back at me. I thought he looked a bit regretful as if he wished he could have kept Jonathan outside a little longer. Then he, too, disappeared inside the church.

I felt weak. My hands were shaking. I looked toward the back door of the Prouty house and saw Mrs. Prouty standing there. She was looking straight at me. She was kneading her apron between her hands and tears were streaming down her face.

She saw me watching her and came down the steps. She walked to the alley, came through the gate and approached. I took off my hat. "Hello, Mrs. Prouty."

She swallowed and raised a hand to wipe away her tears. She said, "Please, Sam. Oh please, don't take him away from us."

"I won't, Mrs. Prouty. I won't."

Her relief was so great I thought she was going to faint. She couldn't seem to speak, but her eyes conveyed her gratitude. She nodded, put out her hands and took one of mine. She squeezed, glanced worriedly at the back door of the church, then turned and hurried down the alley again. At the gate, she turned her head. "God go with you, Sam."

I nodded and watched her hurry up the path to the back door of the house. She disappeared.

I stood there for a long, long time, hoping Prouty and Jonathan would come out, hoping to get another glimpse of him. But they didn't. The sun, now more than halfway up the sky, reminded me that I had not much time. I turned and walked down the alley.

Chapter 8

I had hardly gone past the end of the alley when I heard someone call to me from behind. I turned and saw Jasper Prouty hurrying along, trying to catch up. I stopped to wait for him.

I realized immediately that he had been watching from inside the church, waiting for me to leave. The realization angered me. He could have brought Jonathan out again and taken him back to the house. He could have given me another glimpse of him.

I said, "He's a fine-looking boy."

"Thank you. He's a good boy too."

"And he doesn't know who his father is?"

"How could he? He thinks his name is Prouty."

"How do you explain that to him? When he knows his mother was your daughter?"

"He's only six. It hasn't come up yet."

"And when it does?"

"Maybe by then he'll be old enough."

I stared coldly at him. "Old enough for what? To accept the fact that his father was a killer without trying to be like him?"

Prouty flushed and could not meet my eyes.

I stared at him, trying to force him to look up and meet my glance. Suddenly I realized how unfair I was being to the man. He had taken Jonathan when I abandoned him. He had raised him and with love. What right did I have to complain because he hadn't told him who his father was? Would it have helped the boy to know his father had abandoned him? Would it help him now to know that his father made his living with his gun?

No, it wouldn't. I was the one who should be blamed. I had thought my grief greater than anybody's, but Prouty's grief and that of his wife over the death of their daughter must have been at least as great as mine. I said, "I'm sorry. I

74

have no right to criticize you. You took over what was my responsibility."

Prouty stared at me as if he had never seen me before. We reached Kansas Street a couple of blocks above the saloon and Prouty stopped. He put out his hand and I took it. His grip was firm. "I probably won't see you again. But I wish you luck."

"Thanks."

"Are you sure that I can't help? There's no shame in taking help from a member of your family."

I shook my head. "I'll manage. But thanks for the offer anyway.

He released my hand and turned. He walked back in the direction he had come and did not look back.

Suddenly I felt more alone than ever before in my life. I wanted to run after him. I wanted to stay in Cottonwood Grove and I wanted a hand in raising Jonathan. But it couldn't be. Jess Morgan was coming, as inexorably as death. He would get here sometime today.

I walked down Kansas Street toward the saloon. I supposed it must be midmorning. I knew I should be gone by noon. I'd have to go down and talk to Karl Bruce at the livery stable pretty soon and see if I couldn't trade him out of a horse. I didn't have enough money but I was pretty sure he'd let me send it to him.

Six years, I thought. And it came to this. Beat-up, worn-out boots, a hat most men would throw away and a suit of borrowed clothes. A few dollars in my pocket and a twenty-dollar saddle, my good one having been sold five hundred miles back to pay the difference between a fresh horse and a worn-out one.

I reached the saloon and stepped inside. It seemed dark after the sun-washed street and it was a moment before I could see clearly.

The place seemed awfully full for this time of day. Then I heard the shouts. "Sam! Mr. Court! When the hell did you get back? Good to see you! Where you been all these years? You goin' to stay? Now by God, we'll have a real marshal again!"

They crowded around me, slapping me on the shoulders, clasping my hand, all wanting to buy me a drink. I nodded, and accepted a beer. Dutch Hahn, who owned the Red Dog, was tending bar. He filled a mug and slid it along the bar to me.

I said, "I'm just passing through. I wish I *could* stay, though."

Marv Levy, standing next to me, said loudly enough to be heard over the noise, "I told them, Sam. They know."

The noise suddenly quieted. Joe Peck, who had been a cattle buyer years ago, yelled, "Sure we know, Mr. Court. And we want you to know we're goin' to stand back of you."

Another voice yelled, "Wait a minute! You ain't speakin' for all of us! Maybe some of us want to know exactly what he did. And how many are chasin' him."

I glanced toward the voice. It came from a man maybe four or five years younger than I, with a reckless face and eyes that were sharp and quick. I said, "It don't matter. I'm leaving anyway."

Levy said, "Don't pay any mind to Gifford, Sam. He's always like this."

I shrugged. There was no use letting an argument get started because I wasn't going to stay anyway no matter what these people did or didn't do.

Gifford yelled, "No! By God, let the big man tell us what he's runnin' from! I say we got a right to know."

I looked straight at him. "All right. Over in Wyoming a man started a fight with me. I tried to get out of it but he wouldn't let it drop. Upshot was that he drew on me and I killed him."

Gifford's voice held a sneer. "Just like that, huh? And they're hunting you for it?"

I said, "Not the law. His brother. They happen to be a powerful family."

"How long they been chasin' you?"

"A month."

"A month? For a killing that was self-defense?"

Some of those around me were getting nervous

at the way the conversation was going. A couple or three called to Gifford to shut up. But he would not. He said, "No, by God! Why should I shut up? I say that killing over in Wyoming had to be murder or they wouldn't chase him so goddamn long. I say maybe there's a pretty damn good price on his head. Maybe some of us ought to try and collect that reward."

It was out before I could stop it. "You want to try?" I regretted it immediately, but it was too late.

He studied me speculatively. "Maybe. Maybe I will."

Levy stepped between us. "Wait a minute! That's no way to talk! Floyd, you tell Mr. Court you're sorry."

Gifford scowled at him. "I'll be damned if I will!"

I said, "It don't matter, Mr. Levy. It don't matter. I'll be leaving town around noon."

Others moved in between Gifford and me, forming a wall so that I couldn't even see the man. I understood that they were doing it for me, but I had a hunch Gifford wasn't going to let it drop. I'd seen his kind before and they never let it drop. Not until they were dead.

But I also knew that some day, a Floyd Gifford would come along who would be faster than I was and when he did, it would be me who would die.

The talk went on, friendly talk about things that

had happened in Cottonwood Grove since I went away. Everybody was careful not to ask me about myself. Another group of men formed on the far side of the room around Gifford, most of them men I didn't know. The town was dividing into factions and I didn't like to see that happening.

The group around Gifford left the saloon, except for one or two, who moved into the group surrounding me. Others began to leave, and it wasn't long before the saloon had emptied, except for half a dozen of those who had been my closest friends six years before.

Eventually, even these left, except for Hughie Blake. I was relieved that they had gone. I wasn't used to crowds and they made me nervous.

I finished my beer and Dutch Hahn slid me another one. Hughie said, "Gifford came to town a couple of years after you left, Mr. Court. He's got a big mouth. Don't pay no mind to him."

I nodded and sipped the beer. I ought to get out of town, I thought. Right now, before somebody like Floyd Gifford forced a fight with me. I didn't want to kill anybody in Cottonwood Grove. I didn't want my son to have to live with a thing like that.

I shook Hughie's hand and thanked Dutch Hahn when he refused payment for the beer. I turned and went out into the street.

A wind was blowing along it from the south, stirring dust and a few papers. I didn't see any of the men who had been inside the saloon only moments before and this seemed strange. Shrugging, I headed for the livery barn. The longer I waited, the harder it was going to be.

I'd gone no more than half a block when I heard running steps behind me. I turned and saw a woman hurrying after me. When I turned my head, she called, "Sam! Wait for me!"

Her voice was rich and throaty and I recognized it instantly. She was Lily Bodine, who had owned one of the saloons when I had been here before. It was one of those now boarded up, the Goliad, and I wondered what she was doing now.

She came rushing up to me, her face pink, her eyes giving me a welcome that made me feel warm inside. She took both of my hands in both of hers and cried excitedly, "Sam! Sam Court! Is it really you?"

I grinned. "It's me. How are you, Lil?"

She stepped back to arm's length, without releasing my hands. She said, "You look fine, Sam. You look just fine!"

I said, "Liar. I know what I look like. I look like hell."

She said, "Tired, maybe. And thin. But you look fine to me."

There was a silence, each of us looking into the other's eyes. She started to speak at the same time I did, and both of us stopped simultaneously. Suddenly both of us were laughing.

She moved in close, put her arms around me and hugged me before stepping away again, I asked, "What are you doing now? I see the Goliad is closed."

She smiled faintly. "I'm respectable. I have a dressmaking shop."

I started to say I was surprised the town ladies would let her turn respectable, but I stopped before I got it out. She seemed to know, though, what I had been going to say. She said, "It took a while, but I had some money saved. It might have taken longer if it hadn't been for Rev. Prouty. He brought it up in church several times and after that I began to get some customers. They brought in more and now I'm as busy as I want to be."

I said, "Not married?"

She flushed, but her eyes didn't waver. "I've been waiting for you to come back."

I said, "You have like hell. But it's nice to hear something like that."

She let it drop, but I had the feeling she had meant exactly what she'd said. She asked, "Where are you going? I want you for dinner tonight."

I shook my head. I said, "Livery barn. I'm leaving town again."

Her face looked disappointed but I had the feeling she had known. She asked, "Did you see your boy?"

I nodded.

Suddenly all pretense was gone from her face. "Don't leave, Sam. I know about the men who are chasing you. Make this town stand back of you. God knows they owe that much to you."

I shook my head but she gave me no chance to speak. "I don't remember you as a quitter, Sam." I didn't say anything so she rushed on. "They're up there in the Odd Fellows Hall right now having a meeting about you, trying to decide how to get rid of you before the men who are chasing you arrive."

"I could have saved them the trouble," I said, "if they'd bothered to ask."

"Sam! This town is the best chance you've got. I heard that that Morgan had been chasing you a month. How long do you think you can go on?"

Suddenly the long month's weariness crowded in on me. I faced the prospect of going on, wearing out horses one after the other until the time finally came when I just didn't care any more. I said, "What do you suggest?"

"Go up there, Sam! Tell them you've done nothing wrong and you're claiming the protection of the law!"

"What law?" I asked bitterly. "The marshal?"

"Let him deputize some of the townsmen. Sam, they owe it to you!"

I stared down into her face, tempted. She was

flushed and her eyes were pleading with me, and suddenly I realized how beautiful she was. I nodded. "I'll go up and talk to them."

Lily slumped with relief. Tears brightened her eyes. I turned from her and walked quickly up the street toward the Odd Fellows Hall.

There was nothing for me out there on the trail, everything for me here. I'd be a fool if I didn't fight for it.

Chapter 9

The Odd Fellows Hall was on Kansas Street, two blocks above the Red Dog Saloon. It was upstairs and reached by an outside stairway.

Walking toward it, I considered, for the first time, what it would be like living here again. I stopped at the foot of the stairs, knowing suddenly how impossible a dream it was. The town wouldn't unite behind me. There was no reason why they should. There was no reason why they should risk their lives and property for me.

I started to turn away. I'd only waste my time talking to them. I wouldn't convince anybody.

Then I thought of Lily Bodine. I remembered her face and the look that had been in her eyes. And I realized something I had never realized before. Lily felt more than simple friendliness toward me. Maybe she always had. Certainly that feeling hadn't been born suddenly when she saw me today.

For six years I had mourned for Nell. Now I knew it had been too long. I should have stopped it a long time ago. I should have gone on, the way the Proutys had.

I forced myself to go up the stairs. Lily had said I wasn't a quitter. Maybe she gave me too much credit, but I wasn't going to quit just yet. There might still be a way out. If the whole town refused to surrender me to Jess Morgan, maybe even Jess Morgan would know that he was beat.

I opened the door at the top of the stairs and went inside. Compared with the bright sunlight outside, it was dark and for a moment I could see nothing clearly. Then I saw that the room was more than half full of men. They were seated in folding chairs and it sounded as if everyone was talking at once. In front, on the platform, Floyd Gifford stood, along with a man wearing a star who could only be the marshal, and a couple of others that I didn't know.

Gifford had his hands raised and was yelling for quiet. The quiet came, all right, but it spread away from me the way ripples spread from a stone dropped into a pond. Gifford finally saw me, and for an instant he didn't seem to have anything to say.

I waited, not speaking, just looking at him and

at the others in the room. Some of them had the grace to look sheepish, like boys caught with their hands in the jam. Others, like Mel Dowdy and Glen Sanchez, looked away. Still others looked indignant, the way men do when asked to do something they do not consider right.

If they expected me to help them out, I disappointed them. I just stood there silently and at last Gifford yelled, "So he's here. It makes no difference. Maybe it'll be a good thing if he knows how all of us feel."

Sanchez bawled, "All of us?"

"All right. Most of us."

Sanchez yelled, "You've had your say. Now how about some of the rest of us havin' ours?"

Gifford yelled back, "Sure. Come on up and have your say. Ain't goin' to make no difference, though. Sam Court has got to leave before the men that are chasin' him get here."

Sanchez fought his way through the crowd to the front of the room. He climbed up on the platform and raised his hands. Some of the men in the room jeered and the sound grew in volume. The marshal raised his hands again. "Quiet! Let Glen say what he's got to say!"

The room quieted. Sanchez shouted, "Sam Court saved our town! Not just once but half a dozen times! Some of us owe our lives to him!"

Someone yelled, "So how long are we supposed to pay off for it?"

I didn't recognize the voice, and I couldn't see the man who had spoken.

Sanchez yelled, "If he'd broken the law, it would be different! But he hasn't!"

Gifford shouted, "We only got his word for that!"

Dowdy yelled angrily, "Why don't you just call him a liar to his face?"

Gifford looked straight at me. "Maybe I will. Maybe I will at that!"

I met his glance and then looked away. He'd like nothing better than to force me into a fight. He knew it would be stopped, but just getting me into it would prove the point he was trying to prove, that if I stayed I'd draw trouble to the town the way a magnet draws iron to it.

Besides that, Gifford was too familiar a type for me to accept his challenge until it was forced on me. There was one in every town, a bully boy who fancied himself a gunman and who kept the townspeople half afraid of him and what he might do next. His kind knew that killing a well-known gunfighter would make him a celebrity. One bullet would make him the big man he wanted to be. The trouble was, none of these local bully boys was good enough. They forced the fight, but in the end it was they who died in the dusty street while I went on, with another killing credited to me against my will.

Gifford laughed and said, "Hell, he's like an

old dog that's lost his teeth. All he can do is growl."

Sanchez shouted, "Let's hear from Mr. Court! Let's hear what he's got to say!"

I shook my head. I didn't want to talk. I didn't have the confidence I had once possessed. I'd been chased too far; I'd missed too many meals and had had too little sleep. But more voices called out, urging me to speak. Reluctantly I headed toward the platform through the crowd.

Going on would be easier than this, I thought. Then I remembered the look in Lily Bodine's eyes. I remembered my son, running toward the rear door of the church. And Lily's words kept going through my mind. "You're no quitter, Sam."

I reached the platform. The marshal stuck out his hand. "I'm Hank Jellico. They hired me after you left Cottonwood Grove six years ago."

I took the hand. Its grip was less than hard, and I studied the man's eyes carefully. A limp handshake in a man always made him suspect to me but I'd found out that a weak grip didn't always mean a weak man. Jellico's eyes were expressionless and told me nothing.

He was a tall, bony man, his face seamed from age and weather. His eyes were faded blue, his drooping, thick mustache stained with tobacco juice. Fifty-five, I'd have said he was. Fifty-five and no mean antagonist. I could beat him drawing, but I instinctively knew he'd never fight me that way. He'd find a way to even up the odds.

I turned to face the crowd.

A man yelled, "Let's hear it from you, Mr. Court! You tell us what you did and why those men are chasing you!"

Other voices roared approval of the request. I waited until the room had quieted, "All right." This was hard and going to be harder, but I knew right then that I wanted to stay in Cottonwood Grove—more than I had ever wanted anything. I said, "I was over in Wyoming. I was looking for a job and somebody in a saloon in Cheyenne recognized me."

A voice yelled tauntingly, "What kind of job? Gun job?"

I waited until the jeers had died away. "No. Cow job. Anyway, this young cowboy named Morgan started trying to pick a fight with me. I took it and when I couldn't take it any more, I tried to leave. He told me to turn around or he would shoot me in the back. I turned."

The place was so quiet you could have heard a pin drop. I said, "I told him to let it go, that I didn't want any trouble with him or anybody else. He began to call me names and at last he yanked his gun. He wasn't very fast. I waited as long as I dared and then I shot him. His bullet went through the door about a foot away from my head."

"What did the witnesses say?"

"That he forced the fight and that he drew first. The marshal told me I could go but he warned me I'd better go quick because this Morgan's family would be after me. I went, but they picked up my trail. That was about a month ago."

"And that's all?"

"That's all." I looked at them for a moment, then I left the platform and headed for the door.

Sanchez intercepted me. "Don't go, Mr. Court. Stay. It'll help."

I shook my head. I was angry at the way I'd been put on the defensive and I didn't want to sit here and hear myself called a liar over and over again.

Sanchez said, "It'll help. They'll say things behind your back that they wouldn't say in front of you."

I shrugged. "All right." I sat down in a chair near the door.

I only heard the ensuing argument with a part of my mind. With the rest of it I was seeing Jonathan running toward the rear door of the church. I was seeing Lily Bodine's face and the soft look in her eyes. I was remembering what it had been like living here. . . .

Jellico was yelling, "I'm only one man. I can't handle twenty. It ain't right to ask a man to go up against twenty."

I didn't blame him. But I remembered going up against several hundred to save the town.

Suddenly I didn't care what the marshal's problems were. I didn't want to leave. I didn't want to head out again across the empty plain, to be cold and hungry and wet and tired until Jess Morgan caught up and hanged me or shot me down. Right then I made up my mind that I wasn't going to run again. No matter what.

I got to my feet. I raised my hands, but it was several moments before the room quieted. When it did I yelled, "Argue all you want. It won't change anything. This is my home and I've decided I'm staying here. How you handle Morgan when he comes is up to you. But nothing you can do will make me leave."

There was a shocked silence in the room. Even those who had supported me had nothing to say. I turned and went out the door onto the landing outside.

I stood there for a moment, feeling the weakness that was in me, feeling the weariness. I looked toward the west, half expecting, I suppose, to see Morgan and his men galloping toward the town. But the plain stretched away, empty, as far as the eye could see.

I lifted my right hand and looked at it. It trembled uncontrollably. If I wanted to live out the day, I had better get some rest. I had better ready myself for what I knew I'd face when Morgan came.

I couldn't be shaky when I finally faced Jess

Morgan and his men and I didn't dare be weak.

I headed down the stairs. I'd go to the hotel. With luck, I could get two or three hours' sleep. With that much sleep and with a hot meal inside of me, I'd be more able to face what I was going to have to face.

I'd been selfish when I'd left here six years ago. I'd only been thinking of myself. I supposed I was only thinking of myself right now.

But it is one of man's oldest instincts—the will to survive. Only by staying here did I have a chance to survive.

Chapter 10

I hadn't gone far from the foot of the stairs when I heard the door slam behind and above me. I turned my head.

Karl Bruce was hurrying down the stairs, closely followed by Jasper Prouty and Glen Sanchez. Bruce called, "Wait a minute, Sam."

I stopped. The three approached me hesitantly. I know my expression was stubborn and unyielding because I figured they were going to try and talk me into getting out of town. When they reached me, Bruce said, "I've got a good horse down at the stable, Sam, if you want him. Give me thirty dollars and your horse and he's yours."

I said, "I haven't any use for him."

Bruce looked confused. "I know you said you were staying, but I figured you were just mad."

Prouty was studying my face. He knew I didn't have the money to buy Bruce's horse even if I had wanted to. He said, "I expect you need what money you've got to keep you going until you shake Morgan off. I'll give Karl the money for the horse and you can send it to me."

My face felt hot, both from embarrassment and anger. I was thirty-three years old and all I had to show for it was eight dollars and a gun. I said, "Forget it!" more sharply than I had intended, and I saw Prouty's face darken. I added, "I'm not going anywhere. That's what I told you upstairs and I mean every word of it."

Prouty said, "Sam, you can't . . . they . . . I mean, what about Jonathan?"

"He'll know sooner or later. Maybe it's just as well that he knows now."

"For God's sake . . ."

I looked him coldly in the eye. "If I run, I'm as good as dead. I haven't got a chance. Do you still want me to leave?"

"I don't believe . . ." Prouty stopped. He couldn't meet my eyes.

Sanchez said, "They won't back you, Sam. There ain't more'n half a dozen that will."

"Then they'll see me killed right here on the

street. And as many of Morgan's men as I can take with me."

Prouty said, "Sam, think. There'll be stray bullets flying all up and down the street. Innocent people could get killed."

I looked at him. "You know all the arguments, don't you?"

"Then you'll leave?" he asked hopefully.

"No." I was angry and feeling stubborn. I walked away from them and cut across the street toward the hotel. I figured it must be around ten o'clock. I had a couple of hours, at least, before Morgan could get here. I might have until the middle of the afternoon.

The hotel was just as I remembered it. Outside, it was brown cedar shingles and there was a white-painted veranda that ran the length of the two sides that faced the streets, Kansas and Fifth. There were rockers on the veranda, and above on the second floor there was a balcony.

Usually there were men sitting in the rockers, residents of the hotel and others who had just stopped by to rest and talk. Today the veranda was empty. I went inside.

The lobby floor was of white tile. The lobby furniture was dark and heavy, covered with black leather. Over the counter there was a picture of a wagon train with a pair of placid-looking oxen in the foreground and a man with a wide mustache up on the seat cracking a whip over them.

The clerk, a young man I didn't recognize, came from the office and looked at me. His face lost color. His eyes widened and his glance went to my gun. He started to speak, swallowed and then said, "Good morning, Mr. Court."

I nodded. I guess my anger, still showing in my face and eyes, had frightened him. He shoved the register at me and I picked up the pen, dipped it into the inkwell and wrote my name. I said, "A quiet room. I want to sleep."

"Yes, sir, Mr. Court. Yes, sir. I'll give you number five. That's in the back and you won't get all the noise off the street."

He turned and got the key from one of the cubbyholes. He dropped it on the floor. He picked it up and shoved it across the counter at me. His smile was nervous, and the hand that had held the key shook visibly. I thought what a hell of a thing. You go around scaring kid hotel clerks half out of their wits.

I crossed the lobby and climbed the stairs. I'd been up here a hundred times when I'd lived in Cottonwood Grove and I knew exactly where room five was. I unlocked the door and went inside, locking the door from the inside and leaving the key in the lock.

I sailed my hat at the dresser, then crossed the room and looked out the window. It faced the alley. Below it, there was a shed, maybe eight feet down. If I had to, I could drop out of the window onto that shed roof, and from it to the ground.

I unbuckled my gun belt and laid it on a chair beside the bed with the gun out of the holster, lying where I could instantly put my hand on it. Then I stretched out on the bed.

I closed my eyes. Things seemed to reel and whirl, I was so tired. I had a picture before my eyes of Jonathan, hurrying eagerly to help Prouty in the church. I saw Lily Bodine's face. I tried to summon back a vision of Nell and failed.

Drowsily I thought that maybe it was just as well. Mourning her had brought me to where I was today. Six years was too long to grieve and it was time to stop. Time to think of living again.

Living. Think of living again, I thought bitterly, when death is only hours away from you.

I heard a noise in the hallway outside my door. I tensed, and was instantly wide awake. My hand went out and closed over the grips of my gun.

The footsteps passed and went on down the hall. I relaxed again, or tried to, but I wasn't able to let myself go loose the way I had been before. I kept listening.

I told myself that if I didn't sleep now I'd sleep later and be easy game for Morgan when he came. Or if I left town the way everybody wanted me to, I'd fall asleep out on the prairie and wouldn't wake up until they were standing over me.

A horse and wagon went along the alley, the wagon wheels creaking. I heard the sounds of trash being loaded, then heard the wagon go on again. A fly buzzed against the window monotonously.

I thought back to when I'd left Cottonwood Grove right after Nell's death. I'd ridden away, stunned and angry and bitter and I'd ridden my horse to death. I put him out of his misery with a bullet in the head. Then, carrying my saddle, I went on afoot. First town I reached was one called Cheyenne Wells. First place I hit when I walked into town was the saloon. I put my saddle behind the bar for safekeeping, got a bottle and sat down at a table in the darkest corner in the place.

I took off my boots to ease my aching feet and started in on the bottle. I finished it before it had time to take effect and called for another one. I don't remember finishing the second one. I passed out at the table and I woke up next day in a room upstairs. My gun and belt were hanging on the chair beside the bed. My saddle was on the floor in the middle of the room. There was a receipt on the chair for my money and valuables.

I was fully dressed, the marshal's star, which I had forgotten to remove, still pinned to my vest. That explained the care with which I had been treated. Without it, I'd probably have waked up in jail.

I had a terrible hangover. I pulled on my boots,

splashed some water into my face and went downstairs. I retrieved my money and began drinking again. Next morning I woke up again in the same room, only with a worse hangover than before.

I went on like that for a week. Finally, one morning, my hand shook so badly that I couldn't raise the first drink to my mouth. A man came into the saloon and looked at me and I wanted to hide someplace. I made up my mind right then that whisky wasn't the way for me. I got a meal, kept it down and when I felt able, got a bath and a shave and a new suit of clothes. I bought a horse, saddled up and rode out, still heading west.

I ran out of money in Denver and I took a job riding shotgun on a Butterfield Overland stage running along the Smoky Hill route.

A cowman, riding stage from Dodge City to Denver, offered me a job. He said rustlers were stealing him blind and the law wasn't any help so he figured to take care of it himself.

I took the job because the pay was good. A hundred dollars a month. In Denver, he hired three more men, the kind with hard eyes and guns with the grips worn smooth. The five of us left Denver on horseback for his ranch, which was northeast out of Denver on the Platte.

The ranch was fifteen miles long, and ran back into the foothills for a couple of miles. He had a dozen cowhands and he didn't expect anything from us until someone tried to drive off a bunch of his cattle. We lay around the bunkhouse playing poker and reading old newspapers and magazines. I didn't like the idleness much because it gave me too much time to think.

Finally one afternoon one of the hands rode in to report a bunch of seventy or eighty cattle being driven by three men. The tracks were several days old but men on horseback travel faster than cattle and we didn't worry about not being able to catch up.

The trail led back into the mountains and we figured they were headed for Leadville where cattle could be sold with no questions asked if the price was right. Up there, they'd slaughter them and throw the hides down an old mine shaft where they'd never be found again.

The cowman, whose name was Flynn, said he knew a way of getting ahead of the rustlers. He took us straight up over the high divide and down on the other side and then up over another high pass and finally down into a valley with a clear creek running along the middle. He said the creek was Ten Mile Creek and if there weren't any tracks of cattle here it meant that the rustlers hadn't yet passed this way. We scoured the valley and didn't find any tracks so we made camp on a timbered knoll overlooking the valley and settled down to wait.

Two days later, around noon, we heard cattle bawling in the distance and pretty soon saw the cattle coming up the creek.

Flynn said to stay out of sight until they drew abreast. Then, two of us were to drop in behind the herd. He and the third man would ride out in front. We'd have the rustlers boxed so they couldn't get away. They sure as hell couldn't go up over those high granite peaks on either side.

It worked out the way Flynn had planned it. They tried getting away, but we rode them down. We told them to shuck their guns and they asked Flynn what he was going to do with them. He said what do you usually do with rustlers, that he meant to hang them right here.

That was a mistake, if he really meant to hang them like he said. He should have waited to tell them until after we had their guns. They naturally went for their guns because they didn't have anything to lose.

I beat the other two men Flynn had hired by a full second. I shot two of the rustlers squarely in the chest before the others fired their guns. They both hit the third man. The three rustlers lay there on the ground, two of them dead, the other dying fast.

Flynn looked a little sick. He'd been angry, but I could tell he'd never had a hand in killing men before. It didn't bother the other two, and I was a little surprised to discover it didn't bother me. I'd killed men before, and even though I'd been a lawman before, I didn't see too much difference between that and this. The three had been stealing. Maybe they hadn't deserved to die, but when you're miles from the nearest law, you can't be fussy about how you handle things.

We helped Flynn drive the cattle back. He kept us on for another month and then let us go.

Afterward, it was a succession of jobs like that. I learned that a gun brings a hundred to a hundred and fifty a month. The most you can make punching cows was thirty and your keep.

But the gun jobs never lasted long. A month, or two or three, and then I'd be moving on again.

Gradually, as I went from job to job, my name became well known. I'd go into a strange town and someone would recognize me, and then some young rooster who thought he was pretty good with his gun would try and pick a fight with me. Sometimes I was lucky. I'd get the sheriff or the town marshal to lock the youngster up until I could get out of town. But sometimes it came to a showdown and I'd kill the quarrelsome kid the way I'd killed Jess Morgan's brother up in Wyoming a month ago.

I finally went to sleep. I was so dead tired I didn't hear any of the normal noises I'd have heard if I was awake. What woke me was a loud and determined pounding on my door.

Chapter 11

I sat up, groggy and trying to gather my wits. The pounding went on, but I took a moment to strap on my gun and belt, another to walk to the window and look outside. The position of the shadows in the alley told me it was past noon. It was probably no later than one o'clock, but I had slept nearly three hours and I felt better because of it.

The pounding went on, even louder than it had been at first. I withdrew my gun and stepped to the door, careful to stay well to one side of it. I called, "Who is it, and what do you want?"

"It's Jellico! I want to talk to you!"

"You alone?"

"Hell yes, I'm alone!"

I reached out with my left hand and unlocked the door. I didn't open it. Stepping back, I cocked my revolver and said, "Come on in."

The door opened and Jellico stepped inside. He crossed to the middle of the room and I closed the door but not before I had looked into the hall. Jellico said, "Spooky, ain't you?"

"Being spooky keeps a man alive."

"In your business, I suppose it does."

"In my business?"

"You ain't a lawman any more."

"No." I stared at him. He was nervous and it showed. Without trying to keep the irritation out of my voice I said, "You woke me up but it wasn't to tell me that. What do you want?"

Anger colored his face at the tone I used. He said, "I want to know definitely what you're going to do."

"I said I was going to stay. But I'm not sure."

The marshal met my glance, his jaw tight. "That ain't good enough."

"What do you mean it isn't good enough? I can't tell you what I'm going to do until I know myself."

He squared his shoulders. He said, "I'm telling you to leave."

"*You're* telling me to leave?"

"Yes, sir. I'm telling you to leave."

"And if I don't?"

"I'll have to put you in jail."

"On what charge?"

"Suspicion of murder. You admit you killed this Jess Morgan's brother over in Wyoming."

"If you arrest me, you'll have to defend me against them."

He shook his head. "No, sir. I'll turn you over to them. Then they can take you back to Wyoming to stand trial for what you did."

"I'd never get that far and you damn well know it. If they didn't hang me here in town, they'd hang me right outside of it."

"Then they'd be guilty of murder."

I stared at him. I said softly, "Are you prepared to take me, Mr. Jellico?"

"Not the way you'd like me to. But I'll take you, Mr. Court. One way or another, I'll take you if you stay."

We stared at each other for a long moment, There was a compulsion in him to look away but he stubbornly resisted it. I said, "Get out of here."

He shrugged. "All right, Mr. Court. Have it your way." He turned and left the room. The door slammed thunderously.

I crossed the room and locked it. Then I went to the dresser and poured some water into the wash-basin. I washed and dried my face and ran my fingers through my hair. Suddenly I was ravenous.

I put on my hat and pulled on my boots. I went out, locking the door behind me. I didn't want to come back and find someone waiting for me in my room.

I went downstairs. I could smell food and the smell made me even more hungry. I crossed the lobby to the dining room and went inside.

The place was almost full, but because of the hour, nearly everybody had finished and was getting ready to leave. I stood in the doorway for a moment, watching the way people would look up, recognize me and then quickly look away without nodding or speaking to me. Some of them were the same people who had once told me how much the town of Cottonwood Grove owed me.

But I couldn't really blame them, I supposed. I'd been gone six years and the debt, if there ever had been a debt, had faded. Now they were scared. Morgan and his twenty men frightened them as badly as if they'd been told that Quantrill and his guerrillas were on the way. Over in the corner I saw Mel Dowdy and Glen Sanchez. Unexpectedly they beckoned me, I threaded my way through the tables, more amused than angered at the way people avoided looking up at me. I pulled out a chair and sat down. I put my hat on the empty chair.

Sanchez said, "You look like you got some sleep."

I nodded. "Almost three hours. I feel better."

"What do you want to eat? There's roast beef and . . ."

"Roast beef."

Dowdy raised a hand and beckoned the waitress. She looked at me as if she was afraid I'd bite. Dowdy said, "Some roast beef, Susie, for Mr. Court."

"Yes, sir." She hurried away. I said sourly, "I even scare waitresses."

"She was only eleven when you left."

There was a long, awkward silence. At last Dowdy asked, "Are you really going to stay?"

"Hell, I don't know."

"Did you see your boy?"

I nodded. "For a minute. Prouty brought him out the back door of the house and took him into the back door of the church."

"You didn't talk to him?"

I shook my head. "Prouty says he don't know I'm his pa."

"I can't believe that. You know how kids talk."

I said, "If I stay, I'll see a lot of him. If I go, maybe it's just as well that I didn't talk to him."

The waitress brought my dinner. I asked, "What's your name?"

"Susie Hackett, Mr. Court."

I nodded. "I remember. You live over on the east side of town."

"Yes, sir."

"How's your pa?"

"He's fine, Mr. Court."

"Tell him hello for me."

"Yes, sir, Mr. Court." She hurried away.

I began to eat. The food tasted delicious, but that might have been because I was so hungry.

As I listened to the other men talk, my mind was like a squirrel in a cage, probing, seeking, trying to find some way out of my predicament. In the end, I had no answers. Morgan was coming with twenty armed and determined men. There was no way of getting around that fact. Morgan didn't care about the law. All he wanted was vengeance for his brother's death. All he wanted

105

was me, and he'd have me if I stayed here. What help I'd get from a few loyal friends wouldn't be enough. They'd only sacrifice themselves and in the end Morgan would get me anyway.

I thought ruefully that I'd better make up my mind definitely what I was going to do and soon. Time was getting short and I'd seesawed back and forth enough.

I finished eating. The dining room was almost empty now. I fished a quarter out of my pocket and laid it on the table.

I got up and walked out through the lobby to the street, Dowdy on one side, Sanchez on the other. I looked at the sunny street, at the cottonwoods over in the residential part of town. It was dusty and sleepy, but it was the only real home I'd ever known and I didn't want to leave.

Sanchez asked, "What now?"

"I think I'd better go down to the livery stable and look at the horse Karl Bruce said he had."

Both Dowdy and Sanchez tried not to look relieved, but neither of them quite succeeded. I headed down the street, intending to cut through a vacant lot to the livery barn.

A woman came out of a store half a block ahead of me. I recognized her as Lily Bodine. Maybe it was just coincidence that she came out when she did, but I didn't think so. She approached, her eyes on me, and I stopped and waited for her.

She smiled, but the smile was forced. "Did you get some rest?"

"Uh huh. And a meal."

Her eyes clung almost desperately to my face. "Where are you going now?"

"Livery barn."

"Then you're leaving after all?"

I shook my head. "I still don't know. I guess I'd better make up my mind pretty soon."

"Oh Sam, I wish you could stay!"

"I wish I could too. But the townspeople aren't going to help. They're scared and I guess I can't blame them for that. I'm scared myself."

"It just isn't right!" There was outrage in her voice.

"No." Something I'd heard Jasper Prouty say in church once came suddenly to my mind. "He who lives by the sword shall die by the sword." I'd lived by the gun since the day I took my drovers' wages and bought a gun. Now it was time for that Bible prophecy to come true.

Lily said, "Sam, isn't there *anything* you can do? Won't Hank Jellico help?"

I shook my head. "He tried to arrest me a while ago."

"Arrest you? For what?"

"For the killing up in Wyoming. Said he'd hold me for Morgan and turn me over to him when he came."

"That would be the same as killing you."

"Uh huh. But it would get him off the hook. Later he could always say he'd only done what he thought was right. He'd say he'd had no way of knowing Morgan was going to kill me as soon as he got his hands on me."

"You say he *tried* to arrest you. Did you refuse to go with him?"

I nodded.

"I know him, Sam. He won't give up. One way or another, he'll get you in jail."

"That's what *he* said."

Once more we stood there in silence. There seemed to be nothing more to say. But her eyes, fixed on mine, said much that she had not put into words. I started to turn away, but she stopped me with a light hand on my arm. "Sam, wait."

I faced her again.

"Can't you take the train? Can't you go east and lose yourself? There must be some-place. . . ."

I shook my head.

"I've got some money. You can have it, or I'll go with you." She turned pink as she said that, but her eyes didn't waver.

Suddenly I reached out for her. I pulled her to me and she was warm and eager. When I released her she said breathlessly, "Oh Sam, you'll do it? I can be ready in half an hour. We can catch the two o'clock train."

I shook my head. "No."

"Why? Sam, why not?"

"I know Jess Morgan, that's why. He'll never give up. He'll keep after me. If he wears out himself, he'll hire the Pinkertons. He'll spend everything he's got, if that's what it takes."

"But maybe he wouldn't find us. Maybe . . ."

I said, "We'd live in fear. We'd both know that sooner or later, Morgan or one of his men would show up wherever we were."

"It's better to live in fear than not to live at all!" There were tears now in her eyes.

I stared down at her. The pressure to find a way out was now much greater than it had ever been before.

But what way out? Angrily I turned and tramped across the vacant lot. I could hear Lily weeping softly as I strode away.

Chapter 12

"Better to live in fear than not to live at all." That was what Lily had said. I looked back and saw her standing there forlornly, looking after me.

I reached the alley and turned into it. I felt trapped and angry. I wanted desperately to stay in Cottonwood Grove, but I didn't see how I could. Morgan wouldn't care how many people he killed, getting me. If he had to burn half the town just to create a diversion, he wouldn't hesitate, so long as it resulted in capturing or killing me.

I kicked a tin can savagely. It rattled along the alley. I suppose my state of mind was responsible for dulling my usually sharp senses. I didn't hear them and I didn't see them until they were almost on me. I had no chance to draw my gun, no chance to defend myself. A board held by one of them came crashing down on the back of my head, breaking from the force of the blow, stunning me so that I stumbled forward and went to my knees.

I grabbed for my gun, and managed to get it clear before a kick struck my wrist. The gun fell from my numbed hand and one of my attackers kicked it all the way across the alley. Single-mindedly I clawed after it, only to get another kick squarely in the face.

There were four of them, all young, all looking like cowhands from some nearby ranch. One chortled, "Hell, he ain't so tough! Not for the great Sam Court!"

So they knew who I was. Hank Jellico, the marshal, must have put them on me, I thought. And when they had finished with me they'd haul me off to jail and I'd lay there until Jess Morgan and his twenty men rode into town.

The thought put strength into me. I kept clawing forward, in spite of the kicks and blows that rained down on my back, and I reached a rickety, sagging fence. Ignoring the kicks for a moment, I pulled myself upright, and with the fence at my back, turned to face them. They were four against me but my life depended on my beating them, or at least driving them away.

I'm not exactly a small man, but I had lost a lot of weight. I was weak from lack of food and I was near exhaustion from traveling day and night. I knew instinctively that I'd only waste what strength remained if I tried to fight these four young, strong cowhands with my fists. If I couldn't reach my gun, I'd have to have some other kind of weapon. I was finished otherwise.

Turned a little wary, they edged toward me, although what they thought I could do to them, I have no idea. Perhaps it was the name, Sam Court, that made them afraid. Perhaps they expected me to be more dangerous than I was.

I lunged at them, and they dodged back, and while they were off balance, I whirled and ran along the alley. They were after me instantly, but that moment's respite with the fence at my back, had steadied me. Less than ten feet ahead of the closest one, I raced along the alley, my eyes darting this way and that, looking for something, anything, to even up the odds.

I saw it ahead of me but it was well above my head, sticking in some hay in a loft over a stable. A pitchfork, but it was out of reach. Its handle was a foot above where my outstretched hand could reach.

I turned and ran through a gate beside the building. I slammed inside the stable, now less than half a dozen feet ahead of the nearest of them. I clawed up the ladder to the stable loft.

Hands caught my ankles and dragged me back. I hung onto the ladder rungs with desperation, and yanked one foot free. I kicked with all my strength. My foot caught the one who had hold of my ankle squarely in the mouth and he released me and sat down on the stable floor. I scrambled on up into the loft and through the hay to the pitchfork.

One of them came scrambling up the ladder, with another close behind. I turned to face them, the pitchfork now firmly gripped in my hands.

Always I had been told that attack is the best defense. I let out a high yell of rage. But I also lunged at the nearest man because yelling wasn't going to scare any of these four off. The trouble I was in was deadly serious and half measures weren't going to get me out of it. Savagely, I jabbed with the fork and two of the tines buried themselves in the nearest man's belly, at least four inches deep.

A look of utter surprise came to the man's face first, as if he'd never considered the possibility that he might be the one to get hurt instead of me. Close on the heels of his surprise came a look of pain, and out of this pain came a cry that was very close to a scream. He fell forward against the fork and I yanked to get it out. His weight made that impossible and I was left once more without a weapon. Two of the other three were already in the loft and the fourth was coming up the ladder.

I turned to leap out of the loft to the alley below. In the hurt man's face was now a look of horror, a look I'll not forget if I live to be a hundred. He stared at me and then down at the dirty pitch-fork buried in his belly. He knew that blood poisoning usually resulted from a pitchfork wound and he knew that he was probably going to die.

I leaped. My feet hit the hard-packed alley and I sprawled out as they gave way. Looking once more for a weapon, I clawed to my feet. Bent double, I ran along the alley, off balance but knowing my time was almost gone.

Behind me I heard the feet of the other three as they, too, jumped and hit the alley behind me. Up in the loft, the one who was hurt was moaning and calling vainly to them for help.

I stumbled over an old, splintered singletree lying close against the fence and wondered briefly why I hadn't seen it before. I stopped, almost falling from my own momentum, seized the singletree and whirled.

The closest one was less than ten feet away. I only had time to draw the singletree back, and then swing it toward him. My pursuer had no time to check his forward momentum. He ran into the singletree with almost as much force as I'd been able to give to it.

The sound was a sodden crack as singletree met skull. He crumpled to the ground at my feet without a sound, and afterward lay completely still.

The man behind him hit me with his body, knocking me to the ground, knocking the singletree out of my hands. The fourth one was on me immediately.

Two of them were out of it, but two still were left and I was gasping for breath and shaking as bad as if I had a chill. The singletree was wrenched out of my hands and swung savagely at my head.

It's horrifying to see something coming with that much force and knowing you have no chance of avoiding it. I tried to duck my head but I knew I was too late.

Suddenly my feet were yanked out from under me. The singletree whistled past my head, grazing it. Then I was on the ground, with one man under me and the other above. The singletree, its momentum unchecked by hitting my head, flew out of the hands of the man who had swung it and struck the wooden fence on the far side of the alley.

They were wrestling with me now, trying to subdue me so they could haul me off to Jellico's jail. Both were gasping for breath and both had apparently acquired a healthy respect for me. One grunted, "Get his feet, Rafe, an' I'll try an' hold his hands!"

I doubled my body, drawing knees up close against my chest, with the two still groping and grunting and trying to get firm hold of me. I straightened convulsively, flinging the one who was holding my feet several feet along the dusty alley. Before the other could recover from his surprise, I scrambled away from him, on hands and knees, and plunged along the alley, fighting for footing, in the direction of my fallen gun. If I could reach it and still have time to turn, I would be safe.

Glancing up, I saw a man standing at the alley mouth, a man I instantly recognized as Hank Jellico. I plunged toward him, and he stood there spread-legged, his gun in his hand. I knew he'd use it the minute I got my own gun in my hand.

I saw my gun just ahead and heard the pound of the two men's feet behind. I glanced back to see how much time I had. They were about twenty feet behind. Enough, I thought. Enough, if it weren't for Jellico, standing there ready to shoot me down.

Jellico roared, "Let him get it, boys!" and behind me the two veered away to be out of Jellico's line of fire. That action gave me a little more time than I'd had before. I veered to the far side of the alley and when I was almost abreast of my gun, veered sharply back toward it. I dived, hit the alley sliding and rolled toward the gun. My momentum carried me past it, but not so far that I couldn't reach back and seize its grips.

I was close up against the fence. Instantly Jellico's gun barked at the alley mouth. A bullet tore a furrow not a foot from my head and showered me with dirt. I shoved my own gun out ahead of me and thumbed the hammer back.

But the alley mouth was empty. Jellico had gone, had ducked behind a building.

I turned back toward the two who had been pursuing me. They had also given up and were running across the vacant lot toward Kansas Street. They disappeared.

Until now I'd been so busy trying to survive that I hadn't had time to hurt or to realize what a beating I had absorbed. Now I did.

Every muscle ached. My face was a mass of bruises. My lips were smashed, and one eye had almost swelled shut. My nose was bleeding.

Nor was that all. My ribs were sore where the four had kicked me and one leg would hardly support my weight when I got up. I shoved the gun down into its holster and hung there on the fence, trying to clear my blurred vision, trying to build up the strength I'd need to make it back to the hotel.

Dimly I heard a cry, a woman's cry that was very near a scream. And then I saw Lily Bodine running toward me through the weeds of the vacant lot, holding up her long skirt so that it wouldn't trip her up.

She was weeping with anger and outrage and when she reached me she cried, "Oh Sam! Sam, what have they done to you?"

I was still so out of breath I couldn't speak. I just hung there on the fence, ashamed to have her see me this way. But there wasn't any help for it and besides, I was forced to admit that I needed her. I'd never make it to the hotel and up the stairs without her help. And if Jellico or any of his boys saw me and saw how helpless I was, the advantage I'd gained at such high cost would be lost.

Over on Kansas Street a crowd had gathered now, having heard the shot. They stood there staring, afraid to intervene and help because they didn't know what was going on. Typical and human, I thought sourly, but I needed more than Lily Bodine's help getting to the hotel.

Then a man came from the crowd and hurried across the vacant lot. It was Hughie Blake.

So I knew who my real friends were and surprisingly enough I wasn't bitter because there weren't more. I was only deeply grateful for these two. Hughie looked scared and he spoke to Lily before he spoke to me. "Is he shot?"

Lily turned her glance to my face and I shook my head. Her breath sighed out with relief. She said briskly, "Come on, Hughie. Help me get him home."

I said, "The hotel will do. I'm filthy. I don't want to be messin' up your house."

"Nonsense. You need someone to look after you." Lily supported me from one side, Hughie from the other, and I let go my hold on the fence. I staggered against Lily and almost knocked her down. But she was strong and between them they helped me along the alley.

As we struggled along, Lily asked breathlessly, "How many of them were there, Sam?"

"Four. And Jellico at the end."

"Four?" she said incredulously. "It's a wonder that you're not dead!"

"It is at that," I agreed.

"What made them run away?"

I was straining, trying to keep as much of my weight off her as possible. She was soft, and she smelled good and her arm around my waist was warm. I said, "One of them is in that loft back there with a pitchfork stuck in him. Another's in the alley, unconscious, with a knot on his head. The other two ran because Jellico told them to run. He thought he could shoot me as I grabbed up my gun."

"Then that was the shot I heard?"

"Uh huh."

"And you didn't shoot back at him?"

I grinned and the movement of my lips hurt

like fire. "Never got the chance. Soon's he saw he'd missed, he ducked out of sight."

Lily said bitterly, "That's the kind of law we have in Cottonwood Grove these days."

I wasn't thinking about Jellico. All I could think was that I had been beaten so badly I couldn't ride. And I couldn't fight. It looked like Jellico had won.

Chapter 13

Lily's house was a two-story white frame a block above the hotel and half a block off Kansas Street. A small sign hung in the front window that said, LILY BODINE. DRESSMAKING AND HEMSTITCHING.

We had stopped and rested several times. Now, at the gate, we stopped again. Lily's forehead was damp. Hughie Blake was breathing hard. I was hurting so badly all over that I dreaded each step I took. Lily said, "Just a little more, Sam, and then you can rest."

"All right." We staggered through the gate and on up the walk. We negotiated the two steps to the front door and Lily released me to open it. I leaned against the wall until the door was open. Then, clinging to the doorjamb, I went in.

It was cool inside. This first room was apparently Lily's shop. There was a large worktable covered with dress goods, scissors and patterns. There was a sewing machine beyond, a number of dress forms and a rack of finished or partly finished garments.

Lily and Hughie helped me across the room and through another door. I sank down wearily into a leather-covered chair, ignoring Lily's pleas that I lie down on the couch.

Lily stood in the middle of the room looking at me. There was concern in her eyes. "What are we going to do, Sam?"

Hughie said, "I know what I'm goin' to do. I'm goin' home and get my gun."

He went to the door. I watched him, knowing I should tell him to forget it but also knowing it would probably do no good. The door closed.

Lily said, "Sam."

I said wearily, "Hell, I don't know, Lily. Looks like I've got my tail in a crack. I can't go now and I don't see how I can stay."

"You've got to stay. If you try to ride, they'll catch you before you've gone a dozen miles."

"If I stay, they'll hang me right here in town."

In exasperation, she stared at me. "There's got to be an answer, Sam! There's got to be!"

I didn't feel like moving. I just wanted to sit here because when I moved I hurt. But I knew I couldn't. I stirred and sat up straighter and put my hands on the arms of the chair preparatory to getting up. I said, "First of all, get me a drink."

She left the room. A few moments later she came back, with a bottle and a glass. She poured a stiff drink into the glass and handed it to me.

I put it to my mouth, knowing it was going to hurt. I gulped it quickly, forcing it down. My smashed mouth burned like fire from the whisky and I winced and grimaced with the pain. I said, "Another. Hurry up."

Lily poured another one doubtfully. I gulped it similarly. The pain in my mouth was less this time.

I waited numbly for several moments. The whisky made a warmth in my belly, a warmth that seemed to spread. Finally I forced myself to sit up straight.

It hurt like hell to do so, but I knew the whisky would take over soon, lessening the pain. I asked, "Got any liniment?"

She shook her head. "I can get some. Anything else?"

"Court plaster. Bandages. Laudanum. If I'm going to stay, I've got to be able to move."

"I'll be right back. Go in there and take off your clothes. I'll clean them up."

She hurried out the door. It took a supreme effort, but I got up and went into the other room. I sat down and pulled off my boots. Then I took off the clothes Hughie had provided. They were dirty from rolling in the alley dust and I didn't see how Lily could do much with them.

I stared down at my body. There was an ugly bruise on my belly as big as the palm of my hand. My legs were bruises from one end to the other. There was a bump where my ribs were and I knew I had a broken one. If I got hit there again it would probably come through the skin.

That damned Jellico couldn't have found a way more likely to ensure my defeat at Morgan's hands. He'd had me beaten so that I *couldn't* ride. He didn't want me coming back later to Cottonwood Grove. He wanted me dead, out of the running for the town marshal's job once and for all.

I remembered Lily's remark, "That's the kind of law we have in Cottonwood Grove these days." I'd have to ask her what she had meant. That kind of statement needed explanation.

Lily came back. She came into the room where I was, matter-of-factly ignoring my nakedness. She handed me the bottles, bandages and a towel, then gathered up my clothes. She said, "If you need any help, just call."

I hurt too much to be upset. The door closed. First of all, I took a gulp of the laudanum, trying to hold the size of it to the recommended dosage on the label. Then I uncorked the liniment and began to rub myself with it.

I started first with my right arm, because that was the arm that would save my life if it could be saved. it had been wrenched, and there was a big blue shoulder bruise. I rubbed steadily until the whole arm felt warm. The liniment filled the room with its acrid odor.

As I worked, I thought what a fool I was. Hell, I couldn't have beat Morgan and his twenty men the best day I'd ever lived. Weak and worn out and badly beaten, I wouldn't last ten seconds facing him.

But now there weren't any alternatives. The marshal wouldn't help. Neither would the people of the town. And I couldn't ride, not fast enough or far enough to escape.

All that remained, then, was to stay. But even that was intolerable. Staying, I'd involve Lily and Hughie Blake. My own small son would see my body hanging from a cottonwood, and that sight would leave everlasting scars on him.

Angrily I rubbed liniment onto my bruised legs. Angrily I cursed beneath my breath. I rubbed frantically, as if by doing so I could force the soreness to leave. But it didn't leave. It stayed, only slightly improved by the rubbing and the liniment.

I felt better when I had finished. I hung the towel around me and sat there wearily for a few moments, enjoying the warmth the liniment had put into my sore muscles. I heard a knock on the door and Lily came in again. She handed me my clothes, which had been brushed. My shirt was missing, replaced by a clean white one. I said,

"I've got a broken rib. I'd like to have you wind bandages around me to hold it in place."

"I ought to get the doctor, Sam."

"I don't think there's time. You can do it."

"All right."

I said, "Get some strips of cloth. Anything will do." I grinned. "Just so it hasn't got flowers on it."

She stared at my face. "I'm glad to see that you can joke."

She went out. I put on my underwear and pants, leaving the top half of the underwear hanging. Lily came back and began winding bandages around my ribs. The firmness reduced the pain somewhat and I discovered I was able to move without the rib hurting so.

Putting on the top half of the underwear wasn't easy, but I finally managed it. I washed in the basin of hot water Lily had brought, toweled myself dry and put on the clean shirt. I went out into the other room.

Hughie Blake had hung my gun belt from the back of a chair. I strapped it on. The gun had an awkward, unfamiliar feel.

Lily watched me, worried concern in her eyes. She was thinking I couldn't make it, I knew. I said, "I've been in worse fixes than this and got out of them."

Firmly she said, "You'll get out of this one too."

I studied her. There was a suspicious bright-ness in her eyes and I thought her lower lip was trembling. I said, "You said that Jellico's having me beaten was the kind of law you had in Cottonwood Grove these days. What did you mean?"

"It's the way he gets what he wants. Having people beaten up."

"What do you mean, what he wants?"

"I mean tribute—from every businessman in town. It's not much—ten or fifteen dollars a month. But when he gets it from everyone. . . ."

"And nobody squawks?"

"A few did. They got beaten up, just the way you did. Now the others don't say anything. They pay."

"Even you?"

"I pay him ten dollars every month."

"Why doesn't the town fire him?"

"Don't you think they've tried? He refuses to quit."

"They could quit paying him."

"They could, but they're afraid."

We were interrupted by a knocking on Lily's front door. She left me to answer it and while she was gone, I practiced getting my gun out several times. My ribs hurt when I did, and so did my arm, and I was slow. Too slow.

Still, I didn't suppose my life would depend wholly on speed when Morgan arrived. He had twenty men with him and ten times my speed wouldn't even that kind of odds.

I heard a man's voice talking to Lily. Her voice sounded upset. I shoved my gun back into its holster and walked out through her shop to the door. I didn't limp and I tried not to wince no matter how much I hurt.

Jellico stood just outside the door. Lily turned her head. "He wanted to see you but I told him no."

I said, "It's all right." Lily went back into the house and I faced Jellico at the door. He said, "Jake is in bad shape. He's probably going to die."

"Which one is he?"

"The one you ran the pitchfork in."

"And how about the other one?"

"He hasn't come to yet. Doc says he's got a fractured skull."

I shrugged. "Why come to me with it? You're the one that put them onto me."

"Because I'm going to swear out a warrant for your arrest."

"Unless I get out of town?"

"That's right. Unless you get out of town."

I said, "Get your warrant. But don't count on surprising me again."

He nodded. I could see that he had expected my reply. He turned and went back down the walk, turned and headed back downtown. He did not look back.

Behind me, Lily said, "He's dangerous."

"I know it."

"When you face the man who is after you, you will have Jellico behind you."

"I know that too."

She stood there, hands on hips, frowning at me exasperatedly. "Sam Court, you . . ." She stopped.

"I what?"

"You'd try the patience of a saint."

I said, "If I knew what to do, I'd do it."

"You've got to leave. Or you've got to hide."

"There's no place to hide. Morgan would find me, or Jellico would."

"Then you've got to go."

"I'm too stiff to ride. And too wore out to keep going very long."

"Then take a buggy. Or a wagon. Or take the train."

I shook my head. I realized suddenly that there was more to my decision to stay than I was telling her. I knew as well as she did that if I stayed I didn't have a chance.

But I also knew that run or stay, I was going to get caught and I was going to be killed. And I was tired of running. I was tired of being pursued like some kind of game.

If I had to die, I'd rather it would be quick and I'd rather it would be right here.

I heard some boys yelling down the street a ways. I looked in that direction and saw four boys walking toward Lily's house. They were talking excitedly and looking squarely at the door.

One of them was Jonathan. I ducked quickly back into her parlor so that they wouldn't see me there. But seen or not, they knew that I was here.

Did Jonathan also know I was his father, I wondered. Or had he just come to catch a glimpse of Sam Court, the way the others had?

Chapter 14

The youngsters stopped in front of Lily's house and stared at the front door, whispering excitedly among themselves. For a long time they remained, apparently arguing. I kept my eyes on Jonathan, hoping he wouldn't leave right away. I'd only gotten a short glimpse of him before. Now I watched him hungrily.

He was, I thought, tall for his age. He was slender and his face was tanned from exposure to the sun. At this distance it was hard to tell whether he looked like me, or like Nell, or like neither one of us.

Beside me, Lily whispered, "They know you're here. Do you want me to tell them to go away?"

I shook my head. I was wondering how I could let my son be a witness to my death. I said, "Whatever happens, Lily, do one thing for me."

I think she knew what I was going to ask. "Of course, Sam. What is it you want?"

"Don't let him see me. . . . I mean, if Morgan

comes, keep Jonathan away from where the trouble is."

"I think Rev. Prouty will do that."

"If he doesn't."

"All right, Sam. I promise."

I squeezed her arm. Almost as though I was talking to myself I said, "Fine-looking boy, isn't he?"

"Yes, Sam. He's a fine-looking boy."

"I should never have gone away. Prouty's a good man, but a boy needs a father. I never had one and he hasn't had one either."

"He has one now." Lily's voice sounded strange. I turned my head and looked at her. There were tears in her eyes.

Jonathan left the other boys at the edge of the street and came toward the door. He stopped after a few steps and looked back. The boys said something to him and he came on toward the house again.

He looked scared. His face was pale, his mouth firmly compressed. He hesitated at the door a moment. He glanced longingly back toward his friends. Turning again, he knocked hesitantly on the door. Apparently deciding his knock had not been firm enough, he knocked again.

I looked at Lily helplessly. She said, "I'll go, Sam. I'll see what he wants." I ducked back and she went through the door, into her dress-making shop and through it to the front door.

I was hidden, but I could see and I could hear.

Lily opened the door. Jonathan stared up at her as if he had not believed she would answer his knock. He gulped a couple of times and finally found his voice. "I'm Jonathan."

"Yes, Jonathan. I know."

"I came to see my pa." The voice was shrill and it trembled, but it was strong and determined and, despite the tightness in my throat, I had to smile.

Lily said, "Your pa? Do you mean you want to see Mr. Court?"

"Yes, ma'am. My pa."

"Did Rev. Prouty tell you Mr. Court was your pa?"

"No, ma'am. Chuck did. He said his pa said Mr. Court was my pa and that Mr. Prouty was my grandpa. Can I see him, ma'am?"

"Just a minute, Jonathan. I'll see."

She left the door open and came back to where I stood. She closed the door behind her and put her back to it. "Well, Sam?"

I was the scared one now. I was worse scared of meeting my own son than I was of meeting Jess Morgan and his men. I felt cold. My hands were sweating. I said, "How do I look?"

"You look all right, Sam. You look just fine."

I knew it wasn't true. I'd examined my face in the mirror earlier and it had looked more like raw meat than a face.

But I hadn't promised the Proutys I wouldn't see and talk to Jonathan. I'd only promised I wouldn't take him away from them.

I nodded. Lily was smiling. There still were traces of tears in her eyes. She put her arms around me and hugged briefly, saying, "It's all right, Sam."

I opened the door. Lily said, "Bring him back here, Sam. Then nobody will interrupt."

I nodded. I crossed the dressmaking shop to the outside door. I looked down at the little boy that was my son. I started to speak, stopped, then cleared my throat and said, "Hello, Jonathan."

"Hello, sir." He looked like a scared rabbit, poised to run.

I said, "Come in, Jonathan."

"Yes, sir." He looked back at his friends, whose faces now were awed. He came in and I closed the door behind him. I walked ahead of him to the parlor door and through it. I closed it behind him and motioned to a chair. "Sit down, Jonathan."

"Yes, sir." He perched on the edge of the chair, wringing his hands together nervously. He fixed his glance steadily on the gun hanging at my side.

I was sweating heavily. I glanced toward the door leading to the kitchen, hoping for some support from Lily, but she was nowhere to be seen.

I said, "It took courage to come up to the door the way you did. Did the other boys put you up to it?"

He hesitated. Then he looked up, a nervous smile on his face. "They bet I was scared. They bet I wouldn't do it."

"How much did they bet?"

"A nickel."

"Well, you showed them you weren't scared."

"No, sir. I was scared all right." His grin lost a little of its nervousness. "I'm still scared."

I stared down at him, wondering what you say to a son you've only seen once, to a son you've never talked to before. He looked up at me and the grin faded from his face. For what seemed an eternity we stared into each other's eyes without saying anything.

Suddenly he got up and ran across the room. He ran straight toward me, his face twisting, a sob tearing from his throat.

I dropped to my knees in time to catch him in my arms. He struck me with enough force to almost knock me down, his arms encircling my neck and holding on as if he was never going to let go again.

He buried his face in my chest, and suddenly I realized that my own eyes were blurred, my throat so tight I could hardly breathe.

I picked him up, not even aware of how much it hurt me to do so. I carried him to a rocker and sat down. Holding him, with his head against my chest, I rocked and I stroked his hair and I thought that if I never had anything more, I had at least had this.

After a while he raised his head, knuckled his eyes and asked, "You goin' to stay here now?"

"You want me to?"

He nodded.

I said, "I'm going to try to stay. I'll know for sure today or tomorrow."

He examined the cuts and bruises on my face. "Chuck says you had a fight with some men in the alley a while ago."

"That's true."

"Chuck says he seen two of 'em bein' carried up to Doc Rodgers' office."

"I expect that's true too."

"What was the fight about?"

"About me leaving town."

"Did they want you to go? Or did they want you to stay?"

"They wanted me to go."

"Why?"

I didn't see any sense in lying to him. He'd find out sooner or later anyway. I said, "Some men are after me. They'll be coming here."

"What for? Why are they after you?"

"Because I killed a man."

"A bad man?" he asked hopefully.

"No. Not really a bad man."

"Then why did you kill him if he wasn't bad?"

"He was trying to kill me."

"Why?"

I started to try and explain to him and then

133

realized how impossible it was to explain to a six-year-old the kind of pride that makes men try to kill each other for the sole purpose of building their own reputations, like it was some kind of game that children play. I said, "I suppose he thought I was a bad man, Jonathan."

"Chuck says you've killed a hundred men. He says you're the fastest gun alive."

I said, "That isn't true."

"How many men have you killed?"

I hesitated. I didn't want him to be proud of the fact that I'd killed a good many men. But I wanted him to think well of me.

Lily interrupted us, making it unnecessary for me to answer Jonathan's question. She said, "Rev. and Mrs. Prouty are coming down the street, Sam. Hank Jellico is with them."

I put Jonathan on the floor and got to my feet. I went to the door and peered through.

I could see them coming, Jellico in the lead, Prouty behind, his wife following him. Jellico was scowling. Prouty was red-faced with anger. His wife looked scared.

The boys waiting in front of the house ran when Jellico yelled at them. Lily said, "They know Jonathan is here."

I nodded. I felt Jonathan's hand slipped into mine and I glanced down at him. He was looking up trustingly at me. I knew it wasn't fair that he be punished or even scolded for being here.

He'd done nothing wrong. He couldn't have disobeyed because it was certain Prouty couldn't have told him not to come and see me without also telling him who I was.

I said, "Go out the back door Jonathan, and run straight home."

"I'll see you again, won't I, sir?"

"Yes, Jonathan. You'll see me again."

He released my hand. Lily led him to the back door. I heard the screen door slam.

Lily returned. "He's gone, Sam."

Lily's clock chimed twice. I thought of how much had happened since I rode into town at dawn. I also thought that Morgan and his men should be here by now. They might even now be riding into town.

Most likely it was already too late for me to leave. I'd sacrificed the lead I had on the men who were chasing me. By doing so, I'd sacrificed what little chance I'd had of eluding them.

There was nothing left now but to stay.

Chapter 15

Jellico marched scowling up to Lily's door. He hesitated only a fraction of a second, then opened it and came bursting in. Prouty stood in the doorway behind him. Mrs. Prouty crowded up behind her husband.

Lily positioned herself in the doorway leading to the parlor. Her voice was as cold as ice. "What do you want, Mr. Jellico?"

I knew that if I didn't come out, Jellico would later accuse me of hiding behind a woman's skirts. I excused myself and pushed past Lily.

Jellico tried valiantly to hold my glance. He failed, so he fixed his glance on Lily instead. "You're hidin' that boy," he said. "Mr. Prouty's boy."

Lily raised her eyebrows. "Mr. Prouty's boy?"

Jellico growled, "You know who I mean."

"Do I? I didn't know Mr. Prouty had a boy."

"I mean Jonathan, damn it."

"Watch your language, Mr. Jellico. This is my home. Besides, Rev. Prouty and his wife are present here."

I scowled to keep from laughing. Jellico turned dark red. He stared down at his feet and shuffled them. When he looked up at Lily again, his expression was murderous. He asked, "Where is he, Miss Bodine?"

She said, "I'd suggest you ask Mr. Court. I understand that he's the boy's father. Isn't that true, Rev. Prouty?"

Prouty growled, "If you can call him that. Generally a father sees a boy more'n once by the time he's six."

Jellico glanced at me. Once more he had trouble

meeting my glance. He asked, "Where is he, Mr. Court?"

I shrugged. "I have no idea. I would suppose he is probably at home."

Prouty said, "Oh no he's not."

Jellico said, "He's here. You're hidin' him."

"Did you see him come in here, Mr. Jellico?"

"No, but he was with them boys out front. I seen him with them earlier."

"Then why don't you ask them where he is?"

"They ran, that's why."

I asked, "Why? Are they afraid of you?"

"Not unless they've done somethin' wrong."

"Then maybe they *have* done something wrong. And if they have, you'd better find out what it is. Instead of bothering us."

"You know where that boy is. And I'm goin' to prove you do."

"How?"

"I'm goin' to search this place. An' when I find him, I'm goin' to jail both of you for kidnaping."

"Kidnaping? My own son?"

"He ain't yours. Leastwise, Rev. Prouty here an' his wife are the ones that's been takin' care of him. You got no rights. You seem to think you can ride into town an' just take over. Well you can't. Not that boy, an' not my job."

"Your job? Who said I was after your job?"

"Nobody has to say it. It's plain enough. You was marshal here before an' now you want the job back again. So you can make the town fight your battle with this Morgan fella that's comin' after you."

I said, "I hadn't thought of it, but it's a good idea."

Jellico growled, "I didn't come here to argue. I came to find that boy. You goin' to let me search this place or not?"

Lily said, "Have you a warrant, Mr. Jellico?"

"I don't need no warrant to search the house of no damn saloon . . ." He stopped and licked his lips.

I said, "Go on, Mr. Jellico. Finish what you were saying."

He licked his lips again. I took a step away from Lily, a move whose significance wasn't lost on Jellico. He refused to look at me, but fixed Lily with his stare instead. "Sorry, ma'am," he mumbled. "I didn't mean nothin' disrespectful. But I got to search this place to satisfy Rev. Prouty and his wife, and if you won't let me do it then I'll get a warrant and come back."

Lily shrugged. "Go ahead and search, Mr. Jellico."

I said, "What do you say to the lady, Mr. Jellico?"

He looked briefly at me and I have never seen more hatred in the eyes of anyone. He muttered, "Thanks, Miss Bodine. Thanks for lettin' me search your house."

I supposed I deserved his hatred and I *was* ashamed of the way I had baited him. But he'd started it. He had put those four cowhands on me. He had tried to kill me in the alley before I could bring my own gun to bear and make a fight of it.

Jellico went through the door when Lily stood aside. Prouty looked at Lily and at me apologetically and sidled past, following. Mrs. Prouty kept her eyes downcast as she went through the door. Her skin was pink with embarrassment.

Lily glanced at me. "You shouldn't have done that. He's dangerous enough without making it any worse."

"He can't do more than try to kill me, and he's already done that."

"He can change his tactics. He can shoot you in the back or he can have you killed. It's a mistake to taunt a man like that."

I shrugged. "I know it and I'm sorry. I guess I was still mad about that business in the alley a while ago."

"I know." She smiled. "I didn't mean to scold."

I could hear Jellico and the Proutys going through the house. I went to the door and looked out into the street. I glanced toward the depot, the direction from which Morgan would come, but too many houses were in the way for me to see anything. Lily asked, worriedly, "How long do you think you have?"

"An hour. Not much more than that."

Down at the end of the street, I saw Hughie Blake turn the corner. He was carrying what looked like a shotgun.

Behind me, I could hear the noises Prouty, his wife and Jellico made searching the house. I said, "I'm sorry for their going through your place, but I really can't blame the Proutys much. They're afraid I'm going to take the boy away from them."

"You're his father. It's your right to take him."

I shook my head. "No. I don't figure I've got any rights. Not now at least. If I stay—well maybe I can be a father to him."

Jellico and the Proutys had come downstairs. They searched the kitchen and the porch and returned to the parlor. Jellico looked frustrated but the Proutys had the grace to look ashamed. I felt a little ashamed myself because Jonathan *had* been here, as they had suspected.

Jellico growled, "He was here, wasn't he? He probably ran out the back door when you saw us comin' down the street."

I didn't answer him.

He looked uncomfortably from the Proutys to me and back again. To Prouty he said, "I'll be goin', Reverend. If you need me, I'll be down at the jail."

"Thank you, Mr. Jellico. I'm sorry we troubled you."

"No trouble, Reverend. No trouble at all." He went out through Lily's shop meeting Hughie Blake coming up the walk. I heard him ask, "What's the shotgun for?"

"Figure I might need it."

"You know I don't allow guns in town."

"You goin' to tell that to Morgan when he comes?"

"Maybe he's got a right to carry a gun. Maybe he's chasin' after a murderer."

"I came by Doc's house. He said if I saw you to send you over there."

Jellico nodded and hurried down the walk without pressing the matter of Hughie's gun any further. Hughie came to the door. I asked, "What about Doc? Did he tell you how those two cowhands were?"

"They ain't good. One of 'em's got a busted head and he ain't even woke up yet. Doc says he might not know whether he'll be all right for a day or two."

"What about the other one?"

"Doc says that one is even worse. He said them pitchfork tines most likely will give him blood poisoning, even if they didn't wreck somethin' inside of him."

I could imagine the pain the man was in. Furthermore, it probably was just beginning. Even if he recovered, it would take a long, long time. I'd known of one other case where a man had a pitchfork run into him. That man lost his leg.

But I couldn't feel very sorry for the two. Jellico had paid them for attacking me. They'd taken the money and when they did they'd assumed a risk. If they could, they'd have done as much to me.

What irritated me was that Jellico, who had instigated the attack on me, had got off unhurt. Hughie said, "What are you goin' to do, Mr. Court? I'll help, but you got to tell me what I'm supposed to do."

I said, "Stay out of it, Hughie. I appreciate your help, but you'll only get yourself killed."

Hughie said, "If I point this double-barrel ten gauge at Morgan's head, even he might change his mind."

I stared at him. He was old and he probably hadn't fired a gun for twenty years. One of Morgan's men would cut him down before he could pull the trigger. If I agreed to let him help me, it would be the same as killing him.

I said, "Damn it, are you deaf? I said stay out of it! I've tried bein' nice to you, but it just don't work, does it? All right, I'll lay it out. I don't need your goddamn help. You're old an' shaky and you'll make more trouble for me than you'll get me out of. Now go home and put that stupid gun away."

Hughie looked as if I'd struck him in the face. He stared unbelievingly for a moment. Then his shoulders sagged. He ducked his head and turned. He shuffled down the walk, not looking up and not looking back. He turned toward town.

Lily said, "That was pretty rough."

"Sure it was rough. Do you think I could get him to back off any other way?"

"He might have helped."

"No he wouldn't. He'd try, but when it came to actually pulling the trigger he'd hesitate. Morgan's men won't hesitate."

"Do you think Jonathan went home?"

"You know him better than I do," I said. "Where do you think he went?"

She smiled faintly. "If I was a boy and if my father was in town for the first time, I wouldn't have gone home. I'd have hid out someplace where I could watch."

"I don't want him watching," I said irritably.

"Don't want him watching what? Watching his father killed?"

"I didn't say that."

"But that's what you meant, wasn't it?"

I looked straight at her. I said, "Maybe. I don't figure I've got much chance. But if I should manage to get myself out of it, I wouldn't want him watching and I wouldn't want him where he might catch a stray bullet."

Nervously, I looked at the clock on Lily's wall. It was twenty minutes after two. I'd figured three was the deadline, but I was only guessing. Morgan might be already in town. Or he might not get here until evening.

I had just about decided what I was going to have to do. I'd have to handle it the way I'd handled Burke and his Texans so many years before. Trouble was, this time there was an important difference. Those Texas drovers that had been with Burke had believed in a code of fair play. They had let me face Burke, one to one. Morgan's men wouldn't let such a code of fairness handicap them. They were being paid to take me dead or alive and they wouldn't give me an edge by letting me make it a fight between Morgan and myself.

Lily said softly, "If you had stayed six years ago . . ." and stopped.

I looked at her. I knew what she was thinking. If I had stayed, here where Nell had died, I'd have gotten over it a long time ago. There'd have been time to live again and I wouldn't have killed Morgan's brother in Wyoming and I wouldn't now have Jess Morgan after me.

It seemed natural to put my arms around her. It seemed natural to lower my head and kiss her on the mouth. I didn't want to die.

Chapter 16

It was two-thirty now. Tension was coming over me, a familiar tension that I always experienced before a fight. It made me feel jumpy and irritable, but I knew that it would give my hand greater speed when I finally faced my antagonist.

I said, "Good-by, Lily."

Her glance clung to my face as if she believed she would never see me again. But she wouldn't say good-by. It was too final, I suppose. I went out into the afternoon sunlight, glancing immediately toward the center of town.

I was surprised to see a large group of men turn the corner and come toward me. One of those in front was leading a horse, saddled and ready to go. Behind the saddle was tied a blanket roll, wrapped in a yellow slicker. There also was a sack, probably containing provisions.

I stared at them. Lily came out and stood beside me. Both of us knew immediately what they wanted. They wanted me to leave Cottonwood Grove. The sooner the better. They were even providing me with a horse and with provisions for the trip.

All but two of them were strange to me. One of these, Marv Levy shuffled along at their head.

Floyd Gifford was halfway back, almost lost in the crowd.

They stopped at Lily's gate and I went toward them. Levy looked embarrassed. He said, "I'm sorry, Sam. They wanted someone who knew you to talk to you."

I nodded. "All right. Go ahead."

"They want to ask you to leave town. They want to give you this horse."

I stared straight at him and he looked away. I said, "How about you, Marv?"

He raised his glance and met mine determinedly. He said, "I'll help you, Sam, if you stay. I'll do whatever you tell me to. But I think they're right. I think you ought to go. There aren't enough of us that will help to do you any good."

He was right and I knew it. Hughie Blake had brought his shotgun, offering to help, but I'd known he'd only get himself killed without really helping me. I'd sent him away, humiliating him in the process to make sure he'd go.

I said, "It's too late, Marv. I've lost what lead I had. I've got a better chance if I meet them here."

He looked dismayed. "Sam, the town . . . There'll be stray bullets flying around and somebody could get hurt."

"Then tell 'em to stay off Kansas Street." That was a ridiculous request and both Levy and I knew it was. When the time for the showdown arrived, everybody in Cottonwood Grove would be there on Kansas Street.

"They won't do it, Sam. You know they won't. They'll be watching like it was some kind of spectacle."

"That's their tough luck, then."

"Sam . . ."

I felt my irritability rise. I looked beyond Levy at the men behind him. I said, "Damn it, I'm entitled to the protection of the law. I haven't broken it."

Someone yelled, "We've only got your word for that!"

I said, "That's right. You've only got my word. Do you want to step out here and personally question it?"

That was unfair and I knew it. Nobody was going to step out and face me, knowing what I was and who I was. But they were being unfair too. I *was* entitled to the protection of the law. I was entitled to be tried in a court of law for what Morgan said I had done.

The man did not come forth. But Gifford did. He raised an arm and yelled, "I'll question it, Mr. Court." He pushed through the crowd and stepped out to one side. He stood there alone while those nearest him crowded the others to get away. Gifford said, "I'm questioning your word. What are you going to do about it?"

I looked at him disgustedly. I wondered if he

147

had even the faintest idea how easy it would be for me to kill him where he stood. I doubted if he'd ever fired his gun at another man. I doubted if he'd ever fired at anything but old tin cans.

I said, "Go on back down to the saloon. I'm not going to fight you. Now now. Not any time."

"What's the matter, Mr. Court? Is the great man afraid?"

"I've got more important things on my mind."

"Like Lily Bodine, Mr. Court?"

Beside me, Lily said quickly, "Don't let him provoke you that way, Sam." Her voice was thin and scared.

But he had provoked me. I said, "Later, Gifford, if you still feel the same. Provided Morgan and his boys leave enough of me for you to fight."

"Damn you, I want you for myself."

There was something almost desperate in his voice and I knew how dangerous desperate men could be. He'd made a play in front of all his friends and he wasn't going to let me get out of it. At least not in a way that could be construed as a backdown on his part. I said, "Nothing doing, Gifford. If you kill me, you'll have to shoot me in the back." I turned and looked at Lily. "I'll see you in a little while."

She groped for words. Her face was pale, her eyes panicky. She forced some semblance of calm into her expression. She licked her lips and said softly, "Come for supper, Sam."

I grinned. "Count on it."

I glanced at Gifford as I turned. He stood in a kind of half crouch, his right hand held away from his body and slightly high. He could grab his gun and kill me and never go to jail for it, I realized. And he would, if I gave him the slightest opportunity.

Deliberately I glanced away from him. I looked at Marv Levy. "Was that all you had to say?"

"Yes, Sam. It was all."

"Then I'll be going on downtown."

"Sam."

"What?"

"Take the horse. No matter what happens, take the horse. Your friends bought it for you."

I started to refuse, but something in Levy's face stopped me. Then I understood about the horse. The animal was more than simply a horse. He was an attempt on the part of my friends in Cottonwood Grove to explain why they weren't backing me and why they wouldn't stand with me against Morgan when he came.

They were trying to tell me they weren't fighting men. They were also trying to tell me that they still thought a lot of me, that they would still like to be my friends.

I reached out and took the horse's reins. "Thank you, Marv. Thank the others for me too." I put a foot in the stirrup and swung astride.

Immediately I turned the horse, putting my

back to Gifford, Levy and the crowd. Gifford called, "Damn you, Court . . ." but I didn't turn. Sooner or later he'd force me into a fight but I didn't want it now. I drummed my heels against the horse's sides and the animal, fresh from the stable, broke into a gallop. Behind me Gifford bawled, "Court!" but I was already out of effective pistol range.

Riding down the tree-lined street, I was tempted for a moment to just keep going. I could put a few miles between Morgan and myself. And if I traveled all night, I'd have a little start on him.

Then I shook my head. A month is too long to run and a man gets tired of it. I was tired of running, tired of being afraid. I'd face him, today, here in this town, and I'd either die or I'd somehow beat him and live. Not the way I'd lived for the past six years either, like a predatory animal, but like a man again.

As I turned into Kansas Street, I saw several boys duck into a long passageway between two buildings. One of them was Jonathan. I stopped my horse and called, "Jonathan."

It was a moment before he emerged timidly from the passageway. He looked up at me and said, "Yes, sir?"

"You're supposed to be at home. Your grandfather and grandmother are worried about you."

"Yes, sir. But I wanted to see . . ."

"See what?"

"I wanted to see the fight."

It hadn't crossed his mind that I could lose, that I could be killed. To him I was invincible, unbeatable. I said, "Come here."

Timidly he came. When he reached my horse I leaned over. "Give me your hand."

He reached up his hand and I took it in one of mine. I lifted him until I could reach him with the other hand. Then I put him down in the saddle in front of me. I said, "I'll take you home. And I want you to stay there. Do you understand?"

"Do I have to, sir?"

"You have to. But I'll see you when it's over."

There was a long silence, during which we covered almost a block. At last he said, "Sir?"

I said, "I wish you wouldn't call me sir."

"What should I call you, sir?"

"How about pa?"

"Yes, sir . . . pa."

"What was it you wanted?"

"I was wondering . . . you'll beat them, won't you?"

I've never liked lies. I've never had need of them. But if ever there was a time when a lie was justified, it was now. I said, "I'll beat them, son."

He turned his head and looked up at me. All the confidence and trust in the world were in his eyes.

I reached the church and rode beyond it to the parsonage. I hated to let Jonathan go because I knew the chances were good that I'd never see him again. I started to lift him down, but he turned before I could and put his arms around my neck. I put my hands beneath his arms, lifted him and put him down on the ground.

Prouty had come to the door of the parsonage. Mrs. Prouty stood in the doorway behind him while he came down the walk. I said, "I found Jonathan downtown. I brought him home. See that he stays here, will you?"

"Of course, Sam. Of course we will."

I looked down at Jonathan. "I'll see you later, son. You stay here now, understand?"

"Yes, sir . . . I mean pa."

I turned my horse. Behind me, Prouty called, "Sam."

I swung around. "What?"

"I'm sorry about a while ago." Jonathan reached him and he put a hand on the boy's shoulder.

I said, "It's all right."

He didn't seem to want to let it go at that. He said, "Six years, Sam. His sicknesses, his birthdays . . . all of it. It just plain scared us to death to think you might try taking him away."

"I told you I wouldn't."

"I know, Sam. But when you love a child like we love him, you can't help being scared. Anyway, I'm sorry for what we did."

I repeated, "It's all right. Take good care of Jonathan."

"Good-by Sam." There was something final about the way he said it, as though I was condemned, or already dying. Which, indeed, he thought I was.

I said, "Good-by." I looked at Jonathan once more. His eyes were fixed steadily on me.

I rode away. Before I turned the corner, I looked back. They were still standing there watching me. I raised a hand and waved, and Jonathan waved back.

I turned into Kansas Street, scanning it immediately, looking for horses bunched in front of either the hotel or the saloons. There were a few in front of each, but not enough to be those of Morgan's men. They hadn't come. Not yet.

In front of the Red Dog I drew my horse to a halt. I sat there a moment, not moving, a kind of desperation coming over me. With so much to live for I suddenly couldn't bear the thought of death.

I dismounted and tied the horse. I went into the saloon. At least I felt a little better. The whisky and liniment had done their work. I felt physically able to face Morgan anyway.

Hughie Blake was in the saloon. He looked at me and then let his glance fall away. I felt guilty and I wanted to explain but I couldn't. Now

now. Not until it was over with. If I relented now, Hughie would mix in and get himself killed for his pains.

I walked to the bar and ordered a beer.

Chapter 17

I hadn't felt it when I first walked into the saloon, but now I did. Suppressed excitement, tension. The doors opened and a stream of men came in, men who had been with the group that had, a few minutes before, presented me with the horse and asked me to leave town.

They trooped to the bar, each of them glancing at me and glancing quickly away again. They ordered their drinks, their conversation hushed as if they did not want me to hear.

I was alone, isolated even though I stood at the bar with men on both sides of me. They had left a space on my right, another on my left.

Suddenly two men stepped into those empty spaces. One was Glen Sanchez. The other was Mel Dowdy. Sanchez asked, "Have you seen your boy, Sam?" Earlier he had called me Mr. Court. There was warmth and friendliness in his use now of my given name.

I said, "Uh huh."

"Talk to him?"

"A little."

"Then he knows who you are?"

"He knows."

"Are you going to stay here, Sam?"

I said, "It's too late now to leave."

On my other side, Mel Dowdy said, "Tell us what to do, Sam."

"Stay out of it."

"Sam, these men who are after you won't hesitate a minute about gunning you down. But if they're faced by half a dozen citizens, they'll probably back off. They might get away with killing you, but they can't get away with killing us."

"You don't know them the way I do. Up in Wyoming, Jess Morgan is like God. What he orders done gets done. He's above the law. He's not likely to think things are any different here."

"There's a U. S. Marshal over in Dodge. If Morgan steps out of line we can get the marshal here in less than a day."

"That won't help me. And it won't help those of you who are already dead."

"You can't face him and twenty men alone."

I grinned faintly. "I faced Burke and a bigger bunch of cowhands once."

"That was different. They didn't even know you and they weren't after your hide."

Stubbornly I said, "No."

Dowdy said, "You can't stop us, Sam. You can

tell us to stay out of it until you're blue in the face but you can't make us do it."

I said, "Don't be a pair of fools. You couldn't open up on Morgan first. And unless you could do that, you wouldn't have a chance."

Dutch Hahn, busily serving drinks, stopped in front of me. "Another beer?"

I nodded. He drew another beer and put it in front of me. When I laid a coin on the bar, he pushed it back toward me.

More men came into the saloon. The place, now, was packed. There was a subdued buzz of talk, which I knew was almost exclusively about me.

I began to have second thoughts, to wish that I had left. When I faced Morgan out in the street, everybody in Cottonwood Grove was going to be watching it. If I lost and if I died, I would do it in front of everybody in town.

I glanced at the clock hanging over the back bar. It was almost three o'clock. I realized suddenly that both Dowdy and Sanchez had disappeared. Looking around for them, I discovered that Hughie Blake had also disappeared.

Dave Miller, who had been a cattle buyer when I left Cottonwood Grove, stepped up beside me. "Hello, Sam. Long time no see."

I shook his hand. "Still buying cattle for that Chicago packing house?"

He nodded. "Same old thing. Except that I get 'em from around here nowadays."

For several moments neither of us said anything. Then Miller said, "You're in trouble, aren't you Sam?"

I grinned faintly at him. "I guess you could say that."

"Can I help?"

I didn't answer him immediately. Staring toward the door, I saw Jellico come in. He didn't look at me, but moved through the crowd toward one side of the room. Maybe he hadn't seen me, but I didn't believe it. He knew I was here. I wondered what he intended to do, if anything.

I returned my attention to Miller. "No. I can handle it."

"Twenty men? All by yourself?"

Watching him, I didn't notice the group of men that came crowding in the door. I sensed the movement but I didn't pay any attention to it. There was already a lot of confusion in the room. I suppose that a few more crowding in didn't seem significant.

But I should have paid attention. I should have been paying attention to everything, instead of worrying so exclusively about Jess Morgan and his men.

There was a lot of jostling and shoving, and here and there an angry protest raised. "Hey! What the hell's the matter with you? You can take your turn just like everybody else!"

Some kind of warning made me suddenly go tense. But before I could move, three hard-pushed bodies slammed against me, pinning me to the bar. Miller protested angrily, still unaware of what was going on. But I knew. I felt my arms held and pinned. I felt my gun withdrawn. And I heard one of the men bawl excitedly, "We got him, Mr. Jellico. We got him an' we got his gun!"

I tried struggling, but it was too late. Each of the two who had grabbed me outweighed me by at least fifty pounds. I was helpless as I felt myself being pulled through the crowd toward the door.

Miller was left standing by himself at the bar. My glance caught and held his.

Miller disappeared, my view of him obscured by men coming between the two of us. I let my weight sag against the men holding me and raised my feet to kick out at them, but one of them twisted my right arm viciously and I put my feet down on the floor again. If they wrenched my arm, it might later cost me my life, because it would prevent the efficient use of my gun.

I was dragged through the door and into the street. And suddenly Jellico was there, a thin, triumphant smile on his face. He said, "Now, you son-of-a-bitch, you go to jail. And when this Morgan comes, I'll just turn you over to him."

I think that was one of the most terrible moments of my life. I felt like an utter fool for having let myself be taken so easily. I'd known Jellico had this in mind. He'd tried it earlier when he'd had me attacked in the alley. I guess I just hadn't thought he'd try it in the saloon, though why I hadn't, I have no idea.

Now he'd put me into one of his cells down at the jail and there I'd stay until Morgan took me out. I'd have no chance to defend myself. Morgan would, in fact, probably hang me right here in Cottonwood Grove. Jonathan would see. So would Lily. So would those who were still my friends.

I shrugged fatalistically. My only chance lay in letting them think it was going to be easy—dragging me away. Jellico said, "Go ahead. Take him down to the jail."

The men started away with me, still holding me just as tightly as they had before. The one who had my gun gave it to Jellico. Behind us, men crowded out of the saloon to watch.

I wasn't going to get a chance to break away, I thought. The men who were holding me were afraid and they weren't going to slacken their grip on me until they pushed me into a cell.

A bleak hopelessness came over me. Now, I thought, I could have used the help of my friends, Blake, Sanchez and Dowdy.

We passed an opening between two buildings

and a voice as sharp as a whip called out, "Let him go."

Immediately, those holding me swung around, pushing me between them and the man in the passageway. The man was Glen Sanchez, and he held a shotgun in his hands. One of those holding me said sourly, "Go ahead and shoot. Court will catch most of the charge."

From across the street, another voice called out, "Let him go. Now!"

Over there, Dowdy had a rifle. He was standing on the roof of Sanchez's barbershop. And then, behind Jellico, a third voice called, "Give him back his gun, Mr. Jellico."

That was Hughie Blake, small and dried up, but determined for all that he looked scared.

Jellico spoke to the two men holding me. "Take him on down to the jail. Hell, they won't shoot. They're just trying to run a bluff."

Dowdy the gunsmith leveled the rifle. He put a bullet into the street six inches away from the man holding my right arm. The report rolled along the street, making the men crowding out of the saloon suddenly start crowding back inside again. Dowdy repeated, "Let him go."

The two men released my arms. Jellico started to raise my gun, preparatory to firing it at me, but a second bullet from Dowdy tore up a shower of dirt immediately in front of him. Jellico lowered the gun, held it a minute, then held it out to me.

I stepped to him and took the gun. I knew, right then, that if I didn't kill Jellico I'd have him at my back later on. I shoved the gun back into its holster and said, "You're a yellow-bellied, back-shooting son-of-a-bitch, Mr. Jellico. Now if you've got any guts at all, draw your gun and shoot it out with me. I'll wait until your gun clears the holster before I draw."

The offer tempted him and the insult acted like a prod. But behind the temptation and behind resentment at the insult was a caution that was typical of the man. Jellico wasn't the kind to lay his life on the line, for any reason, if there was another way. He said, "I won't play your game."

I'd suspected that was the answer I would get. I shrugged and stepped aside and Jellico went past me, heading for the jail, the men he had hired to seize me following.

I watched until I was sure he wouldn't still try pulling his gun on me. Then I looked at Sanchez in the passageway. I grinned at him, rubbing my right arm with my left hand where it still hurt from the twisting it had received. I said, "Good thing you don't do what you're told."

He did not reply. Hughie Blake had disappeared. So had Dowdy, from the roof of the barbershop.

Sanchez said, "You can wait over in the barbershop, Sam."

I nodded. I started across the street, stopped when a voice called out from the doorway of the saloon, "Court! Sam Court!"

I didn't turn my head, knowing if I did, I'd catch Gifford's slug in the back before I could swing around and draw.

Gifford yelled, excitement very plain in his voice, "You got an hour to get out of town. After that, I'll shoot you down on sight."

I glanced helplessly at Sanchez. He swung the shotgun. "Don't do anything reckless, Floyd. I've got this gun on you."

I turned around. Gifford stood spread-legged to one side of the doors to the Red Dog Saloon. I didn't know where he'd appeared from so suddenly.

I opened my mouth to tell Sanchez to lower his gun. I knew if I didn't take Gifford up on his challenge now, I'd have him and Jellico both at my back later on.

But I didn't say anything because I knew that fighting Gifford now would be the same as murdering him. Furthermore, my friends and everybody else in town would know it was murder too.

So I'd have Morgan and twenty men in front of me, Jellico and Gifford at my back, along with as many men as they could hire to help them out.

Sanchez was watching me and I had the feeling

he could almost read my mind. Sourly I asked, "Why the hell does there have to be one like him in every town?"

Gifford bawled, "On sight, you hear? As soon as an hour's up!"

I turned my back to him and finished crossing the street. Sanchez kept the shotgun on Gifford until I had gone into the barbershop.

I got up into the barber chair, sat back and let myself go loose. I was tired and discouraged and without any hope. The odds against me were too great. I'd hoped for support in Cottonwood Grove and I'd gotten some. But more than over-shadowing the help I'd get were Jellico and Gifford, either or both of whom would try and shoot me in the back.

Gloomily I stared at the crowd of townsmen milling around in front of the Red Dog Saloon across the street.

Chapter 18

Sanchez came into the barbershop. He looked helpless and he didn't seem to know what to say. He leaned the shotgun against the wall beside the door.

He stared moodily through the window then. Gifford was still standing in front of the saloon. There seemed to be an almost festive air on

Kansas Street. Everybody was just waiting for the action to begin.

Prouty came walking along the street. He stopped and spoke to a man who pointed toward the barbershop. Prouty crossed and came inside. I asked, "Where's Jonathan?"

"He is at home. Mrs. Prouty is making sure that he stays there this time."

I nodded. "Thanks. I'd as soon he didn't see what's going to happen."

Prouty said, "I would like to help."

I could see how much effort it had taken to get out the words. Prouty was a preacher and he probably didn't know one end of a gun from the other. But he did know that "help" meant holding a gun and using it and he was willing to do that for me.

For a moment I didn't know what to say. Finally I managed, "You can't know how much that means to me. But I'm afraid the answer is no. This is something I have to do myself."

"How can you do it by yourself? The marshal is against you and he will hire deputies the way he hired those men who attacked you in the alley earlier."

I said, "I don't know, but I do know I can't involve the people here. None of you know this man who is after me. I do. He'll kill anyone who gets in his way."

Prouty looked worried and troubled but finally

he nodded. He put out his hand. "Good-by, Sam."
He flushed painfully when he realized how that
had sounded.

I took his hand. I gripped it and released it
without saying anything. He went out and Glen
Sanchez followed him. They stood for a moment
talking in front of the barbershop.

I'd reached the point now where I wished to
God that Morgan would come and get it over
with. I'd been waiting all day today, vacillating
between running and staying. Even if I died, I
wanted it over with.

Jonathan was at home. At least he wouldn't
see what happened here. He'd hear about it but
that wasn't the same as actually seeing it.

I wondered where Lily was. I glanced up the
street, hoping she, too, would stay away. I didn't
want her to see me gunned down in the street. I
didn't want her to see what might well happen
afterward. Morgan was capable of stringing me
up right in the middle of Kansas Street even
though I was already dead. Only that kind of
thing would completely satisfy his insatiable
thirst for revenge.

Glen Sanchez came back into the barbershop.
He asked, "Sam, do you want a drink? I've got a
bottle stashed away in one of these bottom
drawers."

I shook my head. I didn't want anything that
would alter the state of readiness that I was in. I

was tense as a fiddlestring and even one drink would relax me dangerously.

I had finally made up my mind what I was going to do. I'd die out there in the street, but before I did I meant to kill Jess Morgan. He'd never run any other men to earth as if they were wild game. And only by killing him could I make sure that my body wouldn't be strung up from some makeshift gallows as a last full measure of his revenge.

Killing him would probably be the most that I could do. By the time I got off a single bullet at Morgan, I'd be riddled, by his men and also by Jellico and Gifford, shooting from behind.

I glanced at the clock. It was three-fifteen. Some of the men across the street had gone back into the saloon. Others stood in small groups, talking and occasionally glancing toward the barbershop.

Lily came walking down the street. She stopped someone and apparently asked where I was because the man pointed at the barbershop. Lily came hurrying across. She came in, and I got up out of the barber chair.

She was pale and her eyes were scared. She said, "Sam, it's not too late to leave."

I hadn't thought about it before, but suddenly I realized how unfair I had been in bringing my trouble home. I had no right to subject Lily to what was going to happen. I had no right to put this kind of memory into young Jonathan, to be lived with as long as he lived himself. An anonymous death somewhere out on the prairie would have been kinder to everyone, even kinder to me, because no one but my killers would have witnessed my death.

My horse still stood tied across the street. I said, "All right. I'll go. I should have left a long time ago." I bent my head and kissed Lily on the mouth. "Good-by. I'll be back as soon as I can."

"Yes, Sam." But she didn't believe it. She believed she was seeing me for the last time.

I turned and stuck out my hand to Glen. "Good-by, Glen."

"Good-by, Sam," he said. "You're doing right."

I released his hand and stepped out the door. I crossed the street, hurrying now, conscious of the need to get out of town quickly before Morgan and his men arrived.

I untied my horse and put a foot into the stirrup. Suddenly, from the direction of the jail, Floyd Gifford bawled, "Hold it, gunfighter! You ain't leavin' until you settle up with me!"

I was partially sheltered behind my horse. I stared toward him, wondering if he could hit me with his revolver at this range. It was a fair chance that he could not, I decided, and tensed once more, readying myself to mount.

Something different stopped me this time. It was the sudden hush that came over all the men standing in the street. I followed the direction of their glances and saw Morgan, accompanied by about twenty men, picking his way across the railroad tracks.

His horse was walking unhurriedly as if Morgan had all the time in the world. He was in the exact center of the street, his men fanned out behind him and on both sides so that the group filled the entire street.

They were like Quantrill's raiders riding into Lawrence during the war, I thought, remembering descriptions of that event related by men who had witnessed it. I took my foot out of the stirrup. Leaving was now out of the question. I'd either have to ride straight toward Morgan, or I'd have to ride the other way, past the jail, subjecting myself to Gifford's and Jellico's attempts to shoot me down.

I led the horse back to the rail and tied him. In an automatic and almost unconscious gesture, I loosened my gun in its holster.

Then I waited, staring toward Morgan, ignoring for the moment the threat of Gifford and Jellico behind. Men came crowding out of the saloon. Silent and awed, they also stared at the approaching horsemen.

Morgan was a big man, his chest like a barrel, his shoulders looking as broad as an ax handle from where I stood. His face was craggy and roughhewn, ugly but strong, dark and weathered from sun and wind. He had a thick, long mane of graying hair and he wore a black, wide-brimmed hat, stained with sweat and dust and shapeless from being soaked repeatedly. There was a rifle shoved down into a saddle scabbard beneath his left leg, its stock sticking out in front but I knew he would rely on the revolver he carried in a holster at his side.

His men carried rifles, held across their saddles in front of them. They still didn't know for sure that I was here. What they did know was that they had better be ready if I was.

Morgan saw me and recognized me while he was still a block away. He halted his horse involuntarily when he did, and for several long moments stared at me as if he didn't believe his eyes.

He turned his head, then, and conferred briefly with his men. Seeing me in plain sight on the street must have rung a warning bell in Jess Morgan's mind. In my place, he would have tried to set a trap. He was wondering now if that was not what I had done.

He came on then, slowly, looking right and left, raising his eyes to the upstairs windows and roofs of the buildings that lined the street. As he came closer, the townsmen crowded back into the saloon. Some went upstairs and I could see them looking out of the dirty second-story windows where the saloon girls used to live.

While he was still a quarter block away, Jess Morgan pulled his horse to a halt again. His bull voice rolled up the street. "Court! Sam Court!"

He could see me and he recognized me so I didn't bother to answer him. He roared, "Throw down your gun! I want you for the murder of my brother Ray."

Still I did not reply. I moved out into the center of the street, however, so that any bullets fired by Morgan's men would go on harmlessly up the street. Morgan roared furiously, "Court! God-damn you, answer me!"

"I'm not going to yell at you! If you want to talk, come closer. Or are you afraid to come closer than you are?"

Even at this distance I could see how that infuriated the man. He touched heels to his horse's sides and came on, despite the called-out protest from one of his men, "Boss, it could be a trap. Sam Court used to be the marshal here."

The arrogance of power was on Jess Morgan like a stain. He was used to riding roughshod over everybody. By now, he didn't even care whether I had killed his brother Ray in self-defense or not. I had committed the unpardonable sin. I had taken something away from him. In this case it was his brother. But he'd have pursued and killed a rustler just as tenaciously.

He kept coming, and stopped finally fifty yards away. Close enough for me to use my revolver,

170

but far enough away so that extreme accuracy would be difficult. At fifty yards, there would be a good chance my first shot would miss. Morgan knew I'd never get a second one.

I'd have liked him closer and decided to try and get him closer if I could. I said, "I didn't murder your brother. It was self-defense. He figured he could get a reputation cheap. He had two men in back of me who were to distract me as Ray pulled his gun. Only I didn't distract. They yelled at me but I shot him before I turned to them."

"You're a liar! I got two witnesses right here with me that say you murdered him." My plan was working. He kneed his horse closer to me as he talked.

"Sure. The two that were in it with him. Tell 'em to step out where I can get a look at them."

"I ain't arguing that with you. You throw down your gun or we'll shoot the legs out from under you. We can hang you with two busted legs just as easy as if your legs was whole." His horse was still moving toward me. Morgan halted him.

I said, "Better have 'em kill me while they've got a chance. If they don't, I'm going to kill you. You're not going to hang me, Morgan. Maybe you'll kill me, but I'm not going to hang."

He grew tense and the men behind him shifted, some of them cautiously moving their rifles, trying to bring them into line without triggering any action from me. They had a healthy respect for me and that was the only reason I was still alive.

There may have been longer moments in my life but I can't remember one. We stood there facing each other, hardly breathing, as tense as two animals ready to charge. I knew I hadn't much chance to come out of it alive. Morgan was beginning to wonder if he hadn't already come too close. He didn't want to die and probably for the first time in his life he was facing death that was imminent. He knew as well as I did that his men were going to kill me. What was worrying him was that first shot that I was certain to get off. He knew I was fast. He also knew I was accurate. His brother Ray had been shot squarely through the heart across the length of the saloon and in bad light.

I have never heard so little sound along Kansas Street, except in the dead of night. No one coughed, or spoke or hardly dared to breathe. The only sounds, for what seemed a full minute, were the shifting of the horses' feet.

I was tense, but I was as ready as I was ever going to get. I *knew* I was going to kill Jess Morgan. I didn't even look at his men. I stared straight at him, or rather straight at the spot on his chest where my bullet was going to go.

Suddenly, behind me, Gifford bawled, "Sam Court! You've still got me to settle with! Turn around and grab your gun or I'll kill you from behind."

Sudden triumph came to Morgan's face. But I didn't turn and I didn't shift my gaze. I still stared at that spot on Morgan's chest. I could still kill him if I did it soon, before Gifford shot me from behind.

Chapter 19

Watching Morgan's face, I saw the uncertainty that had been visible in it before disappear. He'd known as well as I had that I could and would kill him when the shooting started. Now he thought there was a good chance that Gifford would bring me down before I could.

From the other side of the street, also behind me, I heard Jellico shout, "Court! Give up now if you want to live! He wants you for murder and it's my duty to turn you over to him!"

Jellico knew damned well I hadn't murdered Morgan's brother. But this was a never-to-be-repeated opportunity for him to get rid of me once and for all. He had also known that I would probably kill Morgan and he wasn't going to risk the chance that, with Morgan dead, the heart would go out of his men.

In such a situation, seconds stretch out until they seem like minutes. I couldn't have stood there more than ten seconds after Jellico yelled at me. But it seemed like ten minutes, at the very least.

I didn't grab my gun. I didn't dare because I knew that the instant I did, bullets would come at me from three directions. I'd have a pound of lead in me before I hit the ground.

My mind was like an animal in a trap, frantic, seeking some way out. What I did was the result of pure desperation. I couldn't grab my gun. I couldn't run and I didn't dare surrender. That didn't leave me much choice.

I exploded into movement suddenly. I leaped forward, straight toward Morgan's horse. I threw my arms wide and released a shrill shriek, a combination of the old Civil War Rebel yell, an Indian war cry and the scream of a panther.

So unexpected was my action that it took everybody in the street completely by surprise. No guns roared. But that wasn't to say that nothing happened.

Morgan's horse, startled and completely terrified, reared, his eyes showing their whites, snorting with sudden fear. Morgan, settled and tense and expecting to grab for his gun, was caught by surprise. As the horse reared, he fell to the dusty street on his back. The air, expelled from his lungs, made a plainly audible grunt.

I didn't wait to see what he would do, or what his men might do. Drawing my gun, perhaps faster than I ever had before, I whirled, going to one knee as I did.

I had placed Gifford by the sound of his voice. By the same means, I had placed Jellico across the street from him. But Gifford was first because I knew Gifford was tensed and ready to shoot.

He was standing just off the boardwalk in the deep dust of the street. He was half crouched and in motion, his hand going to his gun. It came out of the holster and up, faster than I had expected, but then I had used time whirling and dropping to one knee.

My own gun was out, centering, its hammer back. This was an old, familiar sensation, one I had known many times before. There was, whether I liked admitting it or not, a fine exhilaration to it, a heady sensation I had never experienced in any other way. I had no control over my actions now. They were automatic. I heard the report of my gun and felt it buck against my palm. I saw the effect of the slug's impact on Gifford and knew where it had struck.

Squarely in the middle of his chest it hit, tearing through, getting the corner of his heart. He was flung back as though kicked by a horse. His gun fired, but by the time it did, it was pointed at the sky. He lit on his back. His arms went out and he lay spread-eagled there, dead, not even drawing another breath.

But I hadn't time to worry about Gifford. The instant the bullet left my gun I turned my attention to Jellico, across the street. Jellico had a rifle in his hands, or a shotgun. In that split second, I couldn't tell which one.

I hoped it was a rifle, both for my sake and for the sakes of those who lined the street, watching. Jellico, startled and caught by surprise by the suddenness of Gifford's death, was raising the rifle as I swung my gun and drew the hammer back for my second shot.

Rifle and my revolver fired almost simultaneously and once more, I knew exactly where my bullet went before I saw its effect. But Jellico hit me too. His bullet tore into my upper right leg, the one whose knee was on the ground, dumping me on my side in the dusty street.

Jellico and Gifford were out of it but still I faced Morgan and his twenty men, who now had recovered from their surprise. My gun arm was under my body and my leg felt numb. Morgan was on his feet, gasping for breath and covered with dust, but with his gun in his hand.

I didn't look at any of his men. It wouldn't have done me any good. I shoved my gun hand out ahead of me and, from a prone position on the ground, squeezed the trigger off.

Morgan's bullet struck the street inches in front of my face. Dirt showered over me, filling my mouth and nose and eyes, for the moment blinding me. I'd been sure of the bullets fired at Gifford and at Jellico. I'd known where they had gone. But in the case of this bullet, fired from a prone position on the ground, I could not be so sure.

I got to my knees, holstering my gun, using both hands to try and knuckle the dirt out of my eyes. I was helpless, and knew it, and I waited, tensed, for the slugs of Morgan's men to tear into my body.

I partially cleared my eyes, enough so that I could see through the streaming tears. Half a dozen of Morgan's men had dismounted. They were approaching me, guns drawn and ready.

Better to let them kill me now by gunfire than to let them hang me, I thought. I grabbed for my gun again, but this time I was too late. One of the men, the closest one, kicked out at my arm. His boot caught the elbow, instantly killing all feeling in the arm. I waited helplessly on my knees for them to reach out, seize me and drag me away.

A double-barreled shotgun boomed, first one barrel, then the other immediately afterward. Deep-throated and powerful, the sound halted for an instant all movement in the street.

Thin and shrill and scared, Hughie Blake's voice came down from the rooftop of the Red Dog Saloon, "Let him go! Turn loose of him or the next two loads go right in the middle of you."

He already had fresh shells shoved into the gun and as he spoke, he snapped the action shut, thumbing the hammers back.

Instantly, two of the men seized me and whirled me around so that I formed a shield for them. They knew, and so did I, that Hughie couldn't fire a shotgun at them without also killing me.

He shifted the shotgun muzzle until it covered the men still mounted in the street. "Let him go, or I'll fire right into them!"

One of the men holding me yelled savagely, "Get that one on the roof!"

Maybe one of them would have tried. But another voice, that of Glen Sanchez, came from the roof of the barbershop. "Do what he says. Let him go."

Twenty men, held immobilized by two shotguns. They would probably have tried shooting it out with Blake and Sanchez, but before they could decide, a third voice called out from a doorway just behind them, "Here's another gun that says turn him loose."

Pain was starting now in my leg, replacing the numbness. Blood had soaked my pants and formed a pool in the dust beneath my knee. I felt weak and dizzy, but I knew I couldn't give up yet.

From out of the crowd that had gathered to watch from windows and doorways, other men now stepped, armed, their guns pointing at

Morgan's twenty men. Sanchez called, "Your boss is dead. Load him and get out of town."

Marv Levy knelt beside Jellico. Then he rose and came toward me. He had the marshal's star in his hand and he held it out to me.

I didn't take it right away. I looked around in the street. Maybe they hadn't backed me from the start, but they'd backed me when it counted. Except for them, I'd be dangling from a cotton-wood right now, or on the way to one.

Suddenly I wanted that marshal's star. I wanted it and I wanted what went with it, a chance to live here, to lead a normal life. I took it, and gripped it hard the way a drowning man might grip a rope.

Lily came running across the street. She wasted no time in weeping, although tears were in her eyes. She took one look at my leg and called, "Some of you get him into the barbershop. Some-body go for Doc. Hurry, before he bleeds to death!"

Hands took hold of me and lifted me. I was carried to the barbershop and put down in the barber chair. I lay back and closed my eyes.

My head whirled. I could smell Lily's light perfume and knew that she was close. The marshal's badge was still gripped in my hand.

A knife slit my pants to expose the wound. Compresses went on, pressed hard against the wound and held in place. I opened my eyes. It was Lily who held the compresses in place. But now men came streaming in, and Glen Sanchez took over that chore for her.

Outside in the street, Morgan's men were loading him on his horse. Face down, his hands and feet tied beneath the horse's belly.

It seemed unbelievable, but it was over at last. They'd bury Morgan someplace and they'd go home and I'd never hear from them again.

Lily felt me watching her and glanced at me. She looked at me for a long, long time.

Right then I knew I was going to marry her. I knew I was going to keep the marshal's badge. I knew that I was going to get to know my son. I closed my eyes. I wasn't a hunted animal any more. I was a man again.

About the Author

Lewis B. Patten wrote more than ninety Western novels in thirty years and three of them won Spur Awards from the Western Writers of America and the author himself the Golden Saddleman Award. Indeed, this highlights the most remarkable aspect of his work: not that there is so much of it, but that so much of it is so fine. Patten was born in Denver, Colorado, and served in the U.S. Navy 1933–1937. He was educated at the University of Denver during the war years and became an auditor for the Colorado Department of Revenue during the 1940s. It was in this period that he began contributing significantly to Western pulp magazines, fiction that was from the beginning fresh and unique and revealed Patten's lifelong concern with the sociological and psychological effects of group psychology on the frontier. He became a professional writer at the time of his first novel, *Massacre at White River* (1952). The dominant theme in much of his fiction is the notion of justice, and its opposite, injustice. In his first novel it has to do with exploitation of the Ute Indians, but as he matured as a writer he explored this theme with significant and poignant detail in small towns throughout the early West. Crimes, such as rape or lynching, were often at the centre of his stories. When the values embodied in these small towns are examined closely, they are found to be wanting. Conformity is always easier than taking a stand. Yet, in Patten's view of the American West, there is usually a man or a woman who refuses to conform. Among his finest titles, always a difficult choice, surely are *A Killing at Kiowa* (1972), *Ride a Crooked Trail* (1976), and his many fine contributions to Doubleday's Double D series, including *Villa's Rifles* (1977), *The Law at Cottonwood* (1978), and *Death Rides a Black Horse* (1978). His later books include *Tincup in the Storm Country* (1996), *Trail to Vicksburg* (1997), *Death Rides the Denver Stage* (1999), and *The Woman at Ox-Yoke* (2000).

Center Point Large Print
600 Brooks Road / PO Box 1
Thorndike, ME 04986-0001 USA

(207) 568-3717

US & Canada:
1 800 929-9108
www.centerpointlargeprint.com